"What exact asked abruptly

She would listen, agree and get out fast.

"It's quite simple," Lucas murmured. He hauled her hard against him, his dark head swooped down and his mouth closed over hers. Amber gasped and her briefcase fell from her hand and clattered to the floor.

"You haven't changed," he said huskily. "Still the sexiest girl alive."

"Let me go," she demanded bitterly as she headed for the door.

Lucas smiled, catching her wrist and spinning her back to face him. "The solution is simple—I marry you," he declared, a hint of satisfaction in his voice. "You did ask me once before, remember?"

Amber would have given everything she owned not to. "Over my dead body. Your arrogance is only exceeded by your colossal conceit in daring to ask the question."

"I did not ask a question." His eyes glinted mockingly. "I made a statement of intent."

Legally wed,
But he's never said...
"I love you."

They're...

The series where marriages are made in haste...
and love comes later....

Look out for more Wedlocked! books—
coming soon in Harlequin Presents®!

Jacqueline Baird

MARRIAGE AT HIS CONVENIENCE

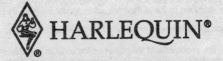

HARLEQUIN®

TORONTO • NEW YORK • LONDON
AMSTERDAM • PARIS • SYDNEY • HAMBURG
STOCKHOLM • ATHENS • TOKYO • MILAN • MADRID
PRAGUE • WARSAW • BUDAPEST • AUCKLAND

ISBN 0-373-12196-2

MARRIAGE AT HIS CONVENIENCE

First North American Publication 2001.

Copyright © 2001 by Jacqueline Baird.

CHAPTER ONE

LUCAS KARADINES stood before the plate-glass window of his New York office, his dark eyes staring out over the Manhattan skyline without really registering the landscape. He ran a long-fingered hand through his night-black hair, a predatory smile curving his sensuous mouth, and a hint of triumph glittered in his eyes. Lunch had been a resounding success; he had done it! Tomorrow afternoon at Karadines London hotel, he and his father Theo, and the head of the Aristides Corporation, Alex Aristides, would sign the deal that would make Karadines one of the largest international hotel chains, and shipping lines in the world.

Like his own father, Alex Aristides was not in the best of health, but unlike his father he had no son to carry on the family business, one of the oldest firms in Greece, hence the sale to Karadines at a discounted price. Tomorrow night a party would be held for the families, the lawyers, and a few friends to celebrate the deal.

Lucas turned back to his desk, his glance falling on the telephone; as for the rest, a brief frown marred the perfect symmetry of his strikingly handsome face. It was time he made the call. He glanced at the gold Rolex on his wrist—at a pinch he could make it back to London tonight. Amber would not mind him arriving in the middle of the night... Amber was a born sensualist—he had never known a sexier woman. Amber with the long golden brown hair, and the long legs; legs that entwined with his as though they were made to match. He felt the familiar stirring in his loins and for a moment felt a flicker of regret.

No, he ruthlessly squashed the wayward thought. There was more to life than wild, white-hot sex. And he hadn't forgotten he'd had to wait a long time for even that the last time he had returned to London a day early. Amber had been at work and when she'd finally returned to the apartment, had only been able to spare half an hour as she'd had a business dinner to attend. They had made up for it later, but Lucas Karadines was not the kind of man to wait around for any woman, or play second fiddle to a woman's career. Several times he had suggested she resign from her job and allow him to keep her, but she had refused.

No, his mind was made up. In fact his decision had been made weeks ago. Lucas had been in the first stages of delicate negotiations to try and buy out the Aristides Corporation when he'd been introduced to the daughter of the owner, and fate had played a hand. Christina, sweet, innocent Christina, was everything he wanted in a wife. She was the opposite of Amber. She had absolutely no desire for a career other than marriage and children. She was Greek with the same cultural background and traditions as himself. And Christina adored him and hung onto his every word. They were totally compatible, and she would make a brilliant wife and mother.

The timing was perfect. After his father's last Angina attack he had confided in Lucas his ambition to see him happily married with a family of his own before he died. Lucas needed no urging to propose to Christina; he was ready to settle down and raise a family. His father was delighted at the deal and the prospect of Lucas marrying was icing on the cake.

Lucas knew he owed everything to his father. He had rescued him at the age of thirteen from the streets of Athens. His mother had left a letter with the Karadineses' lawyers before she died, giving proof that Lucas was the illegitimate son of Theo Karadines. His father had searched for him, found him and taken him into his home, paid for his education, given him his name and moulded him in his own image, for which Lucas was eternally grateful. Lucas's much older half-brother had been killed with his wife in a plane crash when Lucas was twenty-six. Without hesitation his father had made Lucas head of the company and he had repaid him by expanding and increasing their holdings and profits a hundredfold.

He turned, strode to his desk, and picked up the telephone, one long finger jabbing out the number he knew by heart. He straightened his broad shoulders beneath the exquisitely tailored dark blue silk jacket, and shoved his free hand in the pocket of his trousers, and with a look of grim determination on his face he listened to the ringing tone.

Amber Jackson walked back into her office with a dazed look in her lovely eyes and a broad grin on her face. She'd just had lunch with Sir David Janson, the chairman of the merchant bank by the same name, and she was still in a state of shock at what he had revealed to her. The ringing of the telephone brought her back to reality with a jolt. It might be Lucas, and, dashing across to her desk, she picked up the receiver.

'Amber, good I caught you. I'm sorry, but I won't be able to see you tomorrow. It will be Saturday before we can meet, pressure of business, you understand.'

The happy expression that had illuminated Amber's face when she'd picked up the receiver and heard the deep rich tones of her boyfriend's voice turned into a disappointed frown.

'Yes, I understand.' What else could she say? Lucas was

the managing director of his family firm, a large hotel and leisure company, and he spent much of his time travelling between the main offices in Athens and New York, and the various holdings around the world. In the year she had known him, she had accepted the fact he could not be with her all the time. She had a high-powered job herself as a dealer with Brentford's, a large stockbroking firm, and she knew all too well the pressure of work. 'But I'm not very happy,' she added huskily. The sound of his voice alone was enough to make her pulse race, and she was missing him quite madly. 'It is almost two months since I saw you. I was really looking forward to tomorrow—it is the anniversary of our first date and I have some marvellous news for you. You won't believe it.'

'I have some news for you as well,' he drawled, and the trace of sarcasm in his tone wasn't very reassuring. 'But it will keep until Saturday.'

It was not the response she would have liked, but then for the past few weeks Lucas's telephone calls had been few and brief, and her confidence in his love had begun to waver a little. She told herself she was being stupid. He loved her, she knew he did. But she knew the last time he had come back unexpectedly early hoping to surprise her he had been chillingly angry because she had refused to leave her office the moment he'd called and she'd insisted on keeping her work commitments. Later that night he had suggested yet again she give up her job, declaring a man of his wealth did not need a girlfriend who worked. Amber had tried to make a joke out of it, by answering with, 'I will when I am married and pregnant, but not before,' hoping he would take the hint and ask her to marry him. He hadn't. But when Amber had had to go back to work on the Monday he had casually informed her he had to go to New York for a while. The while had stretched into two long months.

Amber was desperate to see him again. She had taken tomorrow, Friday, off work especially to be able to meet him. Now he was saying Saturday, and she could have wept with frustration. But she wanted nothing to upset their reunion, and so she responded with determined good humour.

'Okay, but I miss you. It has been so long and I'm suffering from terrible withdrawal symptoms. I expect you to cure me on sight,' she said throatily.

'Sorry, darling, but it is only one more day—but it might be more if I don't get off this line and back to work.'

The prospect of their reunion being delayed even further was enough for Amber to end the conversation within a minute. She replaced the receiver, her smile somewhat restored at his use of the endearment and his apology for the delay. She had waited so long, she could easily wait another day.

But on leaving the classic old building that housed the prestigious offices of the Brentford brokerage firm, she could not help a pensive sigh escaping. She thought her surprise was special, but would Lucas? Lucas had come into her life like a whirlwind and she'd changed from a serious young woman of twenty-two, who had never worn a designer dress in her life, into the sophisticated, elegant creature she was today. But sometimes when she looked in the mirror she did not recognise herself...

Securing the gaily wrapped parcel she was carrying more firmly under one arm, Amber waved down a passing cab by swinging her briefcase in her other hand. She was completely oblivious to the admiring glances of the dozens of men pouring out of the city office. At five-feet-seven, with a slender but curvaceous body clad in a smart navy suit, the short skirt ending inches above her knees, and the snug-fitting jacket enhancing her tiny waist and the soft swell of her breasts, she was an enchanting picture. She moved with a natural, sensuous grace. Her long light brown hair, gleaming like the colour of polished chestnuts, fell from a centre parting, and was loosely tied at her nape with a pearl clasp, before falling like a silken banner almost to her waist. Her face was a classic oval with high cheekbones, a small straight nose and a wide, full-lipped mouth, but it was her huge eyes, hazel in colour and tinged with gold, shining beneath extravagantly long lashes, that animated her whole face.

'Where to, miss?' The cab stopped at her feet, and with a bright smile she slid into the back seat and gave the driver the address of her friends Tim and Spiro.

She alighted from the taxi outside the door of a small terraced house in Pimlico, and, after paying the fare, she glanced up at the white-painted house. It was hard to believe it was five years ago since she had moved into the house with Tim, a lifelong friend from the small Northumbrian village of Thropton where they'd both been born and brought up. Tim had comforted her when her mother had died when she was seventeen, and he had been in his first year at art college when Amber had been about to start at the London School of Economics. It had been Tim's suggestion she move into the spare room where he stayed. The house actually belonged to Spiro Karadines, a Greek student who was studying English at a language school before going to work at the deluxe London hotel which his family owned to learn the business from the bottom up. He reckoned he needed to let the rooms to students to pay for the upkeep of the house, because his closest relative was an uncle, Lucas Karadines, who controlled his trust fund, and was as mean as sin.

Lucas would not be pleased if he knew Amber was visiting his nephew Spiro, but he had been a good friend to her whatever Lucas thought about him. She rang the bell and waited, a reminiscent smile on her face. It was exactly a year ago tonight, Spiro's twenty-second birthday, when she had first set eyes on Lucas. He had arrived unannounced at the party, and, after a furious argument with Spiro, Lucas had calmed down and accepted a drink.

For Amber it had been love at first sight. She had taken one look at the tall, dark-haired man, incongruously dressed in a house full of motley-clad students in an immaculate grey business suit, and at least a decade older than anyone else, and her heart had turned over. She'd been unable to take her eyes off him; her fascinated gaze had followed him around the room.

Well over six feet tall, broad-shouldered, and long-legged, with thick black hair slightly longer than the present fashion, he'd been *the* most handsome man she had ever seen. Even when it had been obvious he'd been hopelessly out of place in a room where quite a few of the men had been openly gay, he'd exuded a powerful sexuality that had been totally, tauntingly masculine. When his dark eyes had finally rested on her, he'd smiled and she'd blushed scarlet, and when he had casually asked her to have dinner with him the next night she had agreed with alacrity.

Spiro had tried to put her off. He had told her his uncle was a predator of the first order, a shark, who would gobble up a little girl like her for breakfast. He was thirty-five, far too old for her. He liked his women smart and sophisticated—women who knew the score. Amber had replied she was smart, and Spiro had laughed.

'In the brains department, yes, but you dress like—a blue stocking, I believe is your peculiar English term.'

Amber had thumped him, but had ignored Spiro's warning and gone out to dinner with Lucas anyway.

It had been a magical evening. Lucas had asked her all about herself, and she'd responded by telling him her ambition to be a successful investment analyst. How she had just completed her first year at work and was delighted to have earned a huge bonus. She'd even told him she was the only child of an unmarried mother, but he had not been shocked. Finally, when Lucas had seen her to her door he had asked her if she would like to accompany Spiro and Tim to the family villa on the Karadineses' private island of the same name in the Aegean Sea for Easter. Amber had again accepted his invitation. The kiss-on-the-cheek goodnight had been a bit of a let-down. But after questioning Spiro the next day about Lucas, she had blown a few thousand pounds of her first year's bonus in buying a wardrobe full of designer clothes, visiting a beautician, and transforming herself into the sophisticated kind of woman she thought Lucas liked.

By the end of the island holiday, she had met the senior Mr Karadines, and Lucas had no longer been seeing her as a student friend of Spiro, but had been looking at her with blatant male sexual speculation in his dark eyes. On returning to London he had called her and wined and dined her half a dozen times, but the relationship had not developed past a goodnight kiss, admittedly each one more passionate and lingering than the last, but nothing more. Then he had gone to New York on business and she had thought he had forgotten her. Two weeks later he'd been back, and the next dinner date they'd shared she'd ended up in his hotel suite and they'd become lovers.

He was her first and only lover so she had no one to

compare him with, but she did not need to. She knew she had found her soul mate. He only had to look at her and her stomach curled, and when he touched her he ignited a fire, a passion she had never known existed. She had a vivid mental image of his magnificent naked body looming over her, his powerful shoulders and hair-roughened chest, the long, tanned length of him, all straining muscle and sinew as he kissed and caressed her, and taught her the exquisite delight only two people who loved could share. Within a week, at Lucas's insistence, she had moved into the loft apartment he had bought overlooking the Thames, and their relationship had gone from strength to strength. Just thinking about him made her heart pound, and brought a dreamy smile to her face.

'What are you looking so happy about?' Tim's demand brought her out of her reverie.

She looked into the sparkling blue eyes of the blond-haired man holding open the door. 'Happy memories,' she said, and, walking past him, she brushed her lips against his smooth cheek. 'Where is the birthday boy? I have a present for him.'

With the ease of long familiarity Amber strolled into the small living room. 'Happy birthday, Spiro.' She grinned at the slender dark-haired man elegantly reclining on a deep blue satin brocade sofa, and, gently dropping the parcel she was carrying onto his lap, she kicked off her shoes and sat down on the matching sofa opposite.

'My, I am honoured. My esteemed uncle has actually allowed you to visit us. It must be over six months since we saw you,' and, lifting an enquiring eyebrow to his partner, he added, 'or is it more, Tim?'

'Cut the sarcasm, Spiro. Amber is our friend, even if we do abhor her taste in men. Open your gift.'

'Yes, Spiro, where Lucas is concerned we've agreed to

differ. So open the present—I'll have you know I went to great trouble to find just the right gift,' Amber declared with a grin.

'So-rry, Amber,' he drawled dramatically. 'You've caught me in a bad mood; I am finally beginning to feel my age.'

'At twenty-three!' she exclaimed. 'Don't make me laugh.'

'You deserve to laugh, Amber. You deserve to be happy,' Spiro suddenly said seriously.

'I am happy.' She grinned back. 'Now open the parcel.'

Two minutes later Spiro was on his feet and pressing a swift kiss on Amber's cheek. 'I love it, Amber,' he said, his gaze straying back to the small sketch of two young men, clad in loincloths, facing up as if to wrestle. 'But it must have cost you a fortune—it is an original from the nineteenth century, isn't it?'

'Of course, I would not dare give you a fake,' she replied, and all three laughed. Amber knew Spiro hated working for the family firm and his burning ambition was to set up his own art gallery.

Unfortunately she also knew Lucas controlled the purse strings, and Spiro could not inherit his late father's share of the firm until he was twenty-five, or married. Spiro had a very generous monthly allowance, but he spent every penny.

The week after she'd moved in with Lucas, she had tried to put Spiro's point of view to Lucas but he had withdrawn behind a cold, impenetrable mask and told her curtly to keep out of their family business, and also suggested she keep away from his nephew.

The ease with which he had turned into a hard, remote stranger as though her thoughts and opinions were nothing had scared her. Amber had wanted to argue, she'd tried, but Lucas had simply blanked her. Unfortunately it had put a strain on Amber's friendship with her former flatmates. She did keep in touch with Tim on a regular basis—they talked on the phone every week or so—but Spiro was right. It was months since she had seen them both.

'I bet my uncle does not know you spent a fortune on this for me?' Spiro said, propping the framed sketch on the cast-iron mantelpiece, before turning back to look down on Amber.

'It has nothing to do with Lucas. I found out two weeks ago my bonus at the end of this financial year, on the fifth of April, is—wait for it, boys,' and with a wide grin, she said, 'almost a quarter of a million.'

'Well done, Amber, love,' Tim exclaimed. 'I always knew you were a genius.'

'This calls for a double celebration! Break out the bubbly, Tim, and let the party start,' Spiro added his congratulations. 'The three musketeers are back in action.'

Moisture glazed Amber's eyes at Spiro's reminder of what the three of them used to be nicknamed by their friends when they had all lived together. She'd changed and moved on, and the carefree days were long gone, but not forgotten.

The champagne was produced and toasts drank to Spiro, to Amber, to Tim, to life, and anything else they could think of. It was like old times.

Two hours later, her jacket long since removed and the clip taken from her hair, Amber was curled up on the sofa with a glass of champagne in her hand when Spiro dropped a bomb on the proceedings.

'So, Amber, what do you think of this idea of Lucas's to get married? I saw Grandfather yesterday—he is staying at the hotel while having a check-up at his Harley Street doctor, and he is delighted at the news.'

Suddenly the world seemed a wonderful place to Amber, even in her half-inebriated state. 'He told you that? Lucas is thinking of getting married! I can't believe it!' she cried happily. Lucas had actually told his father they were getting married; she couldn't wait for him to get home to ask her. Of course, she would have to pretend she didn't know. 'I spoke to Lucas this afternoon and I was disappointed because he can't make it back from New York until Saturday.' Her golden eyes sparkled like jewels in her flushed face. 'But he did say he had some news for me, and I never guessed.' Her not-so-subtle hint about giving up work when she was married and pregnant had obviously worked after all, she thought ecstatically.

'According to Grandfather, Lucas has news for you, all right, but—' Spiro started to speak but was cut off in midflow by Tim.

'Shut up, Spiro. Amber does not need to know second hand.'

'Please, Spiro, tell me what your grandfather said. I have only met him the one time we were all in Greece but I thought he liked me.'

A harsh laugh escaped Spiro. 'Oh, he likes you, all right, but not for what you think.'

'Spiro, no. It is none of your business,' Tim interjected again. 'We are having a good time—leave it.'

'Why? Amber has been our friend for years—she deserves to know the truth. Do you really want her to find out cold?'

Lost in her dream of wedded bliss, she was only half listening but it slowly began to dawn on Amber that the two men were arguing. 'What's the matter?' She glanced from one to the other. They looked serious. Straightening up in the seat, she drained her glass and placed it on the floor at her feet. 'Come on, guys, find *what* out cold?' she demanded cheerfully.

The two men looked at each other, and then Tim nodded. 'You're right, she deserves better.'

'Better than what?' Amber queried.

Spiro jumped to his feet. 'Better than my bastard of an uncle.'

'Oh, please, Spiro, not that again. Why can't you just be happy that Lucas and I love each other? We accept you and Tim are partners, why can't you return the favour and accept Lucas and I are partners just the same, instead of bleating on about him being a bastard?'

When she'd first told Tim and Spiro she was moving out to set up home with Lucas, Spiro had tried all ways to get her to change her mind. Finally, in a rage, he'd told her Lucas was the illegitimate child of his grandfather, and his mother was little better than a prostitute, notorious in Athens for her string of lovers, and Lucas was no better. Amber had refused to listen then and she refused to listen now. 'In case you've forgotten, I never knew my father. So what does that make me?'

Spiro, his anger subsiding, looked at her with glistening brown eyes full of compassion. 'I didn't mean it literally, though that is true. I meant it figuratively, Amber. Lucas does not consider you his partner. He considers you his mistress, nothing more, and easily dispensable.'

'Only married men have mistresses, Spiro,' Amber snapped back. 'You know nothing about my relationship with Lucas.' Her face paled at Spiro's hurtful comments. 'And I think it's time I left.' Rising unsteadily to her feet, she glanced down at her old friends. Tim was watching her with compassion, and that hurt more than anything else did. Tim had known her since infant school, surely she should be able to count on his support? But apparently not.

'Listen to Spiro, Amber. It's for your own good,' Tim said quietly.

'Lucas is good for me and to me, and that is all I need to know.' Picking up her purse, she slipped her shoes back on her feet.

'Wait, Amber.' Spiro stood up and caught her arm as she would have moved towards the door. 'You are a lovely, highly intelligent girl, with a genius for picking winners in the money markets, but you're hopelessly naive where men are concerned. Lucas is the only man you have ever known.'

'He is the only man I want to know. Now, let go of my arm.'

Reluctantly Spiro let her go. 'Just one more thing, Amber. I know who Lucas intends marrying, and it is not—'

Amber cut in angrily. 'I am not listening to any more of this,' an inexplicable fear made her yell. Spiro was half drunk and he was lying, he had to be. 'You're lying, and I know why—you can't bear to see Lucas and I happy together. You want to hurt Lucas by trying to break us up, just because he won't give you your inheritance ahead of time. I can read you like a book, Spiro, you have to dominate everyone around you. Tim might be happy to let you get away with it, but Lucas won't and that is what sticks in your craw. Grow up, why don't you?'

Spiro shook his dark head. 'You're blind, Amber, plain blind.' His dark eyes sought Tim's, his exasperation showing. 'Now what?'

Tim grimaced. 'Give it up, Spiro, she will never believe you.'

'All right, Amber, think what you like.' Spiro held his hands up in front of him. 'But do me one favour—I am dining with my grandfather at the hotel tomorrow night. He is having a bit of a party to celebrate a business deal and hopefully his return to good health. He has asked me to bring you along, and, as you say Lucas will not be back until Saturday, there is nothing to stop you. Will you come?'

Amber was torn. She didn't want to go anywhere with Spiro, but on the other hand... 'Your grandfather actually asked you to invite me?' she queried.

'Yes, in fact he was insistent.'

'In that case, yes.' How kind of him, Amber thought, the old man must know Lucas was not in London, and so had asked Spiro to bring her to his party.

'Good, I'll pick you up at your place at eight.' She never saw the gleam of determination in Spiro's eyes, that made him look uncannily like his uncle for a fleeting instant, as she said her goodbyes and left.

Later that night as she slipped a satin nightgown over her head she walked restlessly around the large bedroom she shared with Lucas. Spiro's bitchy words had upset her more than she wanted to admit. She slid open one of the wardrobe doors that lined two walls, and let her hand trail across the fine fabric of a couple of Lucas's tailored suits. The faintest lingering trace of his cologne teased her nostrils, and somehow she was reassured. Lucas loved her, she knew he did, and on that thought she climbed into the king-sized bed and sleep claimed her.

Amber glanced at her reflection for the last time in the large mirrored doors of the wardrobes that formed one wall of the bedroom. She looked good, better than good. Great, she told herself. Her hair was washed and brushed until it shone dark gold, and she had clipped the sides up into a coronet on top of her head, while the rest fell down her back like a swathe of silk. She had opted for a classic black DKNY dress—the fine black silk jersey clung to her body like a second skin, the sleeves long and fitted, the skirt ending inches above her knees. The low-cut square neckline exposed the gentle curve of her firm breasts, setting off to perfection the emerald and diamond necklace she had clasped around her throat. The matching drop earrings glinted against the swan-like elegance of her neck. Both had been presents from Lucas. On her feet she wore three-inch-heeled black sandals, adding to her already tall stature.

Picking up her purse and a jade-green pashmina shawl, she walked down the spiral staircase to the vast floor area of the apartment. She loved the polished hardwood floor, and the carefully arranged sofas that picked out the colour in the cashmere rug. In fact she loved her home. But where was Spiro? He was ten minutes late.

She crossed the room to a large desk, her hand reaching out for the telephone. She would try one last time to ring Lucas in New York. Picking up the instrument, she dialled the number. Two minutes later she replaced the receiver, the same reply as she had got earlier echoing in her head. 'I'm sorry but Mr Karadines is not in the office today, if you would like to leave a message...' She had also tried his suite at the Karadines Hotel in New York, and got no reply.

The bell rang and she had no time to worry where Lucas was. Spiro had arrived.

Two minutes later she was seated in the back of a taxi-cab with Spiro looking very elegant in a conservative black dinner suit and white shirt; the only hint at his rebellious personality was a vibrantly striped bow-tie in red, green and blue.

'You look rather nice,' Amber said with a grin. 'Though I don't know about the bow-tie.'

'And you, dear girl, look as stunning as ever.' But there was no smile in his eyes as he reached out and caught both of Amber's hands in his.

'Where to now, Gov?' the taxi driver asked.

'Hold it a minute or two,' Spiro responded, then, glancing back at Amber, he added, 'You must listen to me and believe me. Tim made me promise that I would tell you before we arrive at the hotel so if you want to cancel you can do so. I am sorry, truly sorry, Amber, but Lucas will be at the party.'

Her hands jerked in his hold but he did not set her free. His brown eyes held hers, and there was no doubting the sincerity and sadness in their depths.

'How...?' All the blood drained from her face. 'How do you know?' she asked quietly.

'Because, a rare occurrence for me, I admit, I actually went to work for a few hours this afternoon in my capacity of Assistant Manager at the hotel. I saw Lucas arriving with two guests, Alex Aristides and his young daughter Christina. They went to Grandfather's suite. Ten minutes later I escorted the two family lawyers to the same suite. Karadines have bought out the Aristides Corporation. The deal was signed this afternoon. Needless to say they didn't need my signature, although I own half the company. My trustees did it for me. I was given the task of amusing the teenage daughter for an hour. An hour spent standing around in the boutiques in the hotel lobby. The girl could shop for the world.'

'So it was business—Lucas said he was tied up with business, he would not lie to me,' she declared adamantly. Though he had lied by omission—he had led her to believe he was staying in New York...

'Stop, Amber.' Spiro squeezed her hands in his. 'Please don't do this to yourself. Christina Aristides is eighteen years of age and obviously part of the deal.'

'No, no, Spiro, you're wrong. Lucas would never do that to me,' Amber said firmly, but deep down inside a tiny voice of dissent was telling her he might.

'He is a chip off the old block, as you English say. How do you think Grandfather made his money? As a young man he went to sea on a cruise liner as a waiter. Twelve months later he married the owner's daughter, a woman ten years older than him, but for a waiter that was some step up. To give him his due, under his control the firm went from strength to strength. But my grandmother was no fool—she knew he had several mistresses and Lucas's mother was one of them. So she kept the stock in her name, and on her death half went to Grandfather and half to her son, my father. Do you really think Grandfather would have risked his whole business on taking Lucas in, and giving him his name, if my grandmother had still been alive? My parents did not object because they already had half the business.'

'But that does not mean Lucas would marry for money. He does not need to,' she defended him staunchly.

'Amber, Grandfather wants this deal, and Lucas is exactly like him. They are both very Greek, very traditional. Everything is business to them. Lucas will marry the girl. You have no chance, Amber. Believe me, you never did.'

'You don't know Lucas as I do. He might just be stringing the girl along until the deal was signed…' She stopped, realising how desperate she sounded, as if she would rather think of Lucas as a ruthless, manipulative businessman than face the fact he might leave her.

'Well, I suppose it is a possibility and if that is what

you want to believe...' Spiro shrugged his broad shoulders...'we might as well go.'

'You say Tim told you to tell me this.' She looked at Spiro with icy eyes. 'I don't believe you. Tim would never be so cruel.'

'You're right, of course—Tim has not a cruel bone in his body. I, on the other hand, wanted to walk you straight into the party and let you come face to face with Lucas. In fact I was hoping you would cause a scene in front of my grandfather. Then my precious uncle would be seen for the devil he is, but Tim would not let me.'

'You actually believe all you are telling me,' Amber whispered, the full horror of Spiro's revelation finally sinking into her troubled mind.

'You don't have to take my word. You can go back into your apartment and bury your head in the sand like an ostrich for one more night. Or you can come with me and see for yourself.' A challenging smile curved his full lips. 'If you have the nerve.'

Amber had never refused a challenge in her life and she was not going to start now. Besides which, she did not believe Spiro. Her heart would not let her...

CHAPTER TWO

AMBER, tall and sophisticated in the black silk dress with jewels gleaming at her throat, handed her shawl in to the cloakroom attendant, and turned back to Spiro.

'Ready.' She smiled. Spiro had to be mistaken, she told herself yet again, her golden eyes straying to the wide open doors of the private function room where the party was being held.

'Take my arm, Amber.' Spiro picked up her nerveless hand and slipped it through his arm as they walked into the elegant room.

Lucas Karadines saw Amber before she had even got through the door. She looked sensational. Shock held him rigid for a second, then he looked away hastily but not before seeing her companion, Spiro! Lucas's black eyes closed briefly. Oh, hell! He almost groaned out loud. For the first time in his adult life he felt about two inches tall. He knew deep down he should have made the effort to see Amber some time today and finish their relationship, but he had been reluctant to do so. But what the hell was she doing here? He did not need to ask. Spiro, of course. Spiro would find it amusing.

He felt a tug on his sleeve, and looked down into the round open face of Christina. Thank God his betrothal to Christina was not to be announced until next week—at least that would give him time to explain to Amber. He would not wish to hurt her for the world. His dark eyes were fixed on Christina, but more worrying was that in his mind's eye he was seeing the stunningly sensual naked figure of Amber, the night he had given her the necklace as a birthday present, the emeralds blazing around her neck her only adornment. Brutally he squashed the image, much the way he would like to squash Spiro for putting him in this position. Determinedly he smiled down at Christina, and, slipping an arm around her shoulder, continued the conversation with their respective fathers.

Amber's golden gaze urgently scanned the crowded room, hoping against hope she would not find the man she was looking for. Then she spotted Lucas. It was two long months since she had seen him, and she could not help it as her eyes drank in the sight of him. Why he was here instead of New York didn't matter, he was here…now…

He was the tallest, sexiest man in the room. His superbly muscled frame was clad in a black dinner suit, the exquisitely tailored jacket fitted perfectly across his broad shoulders, the pure white of the dress shirt he wore contrasted starkly with his bronzed skin. Her heart squeezed in her chest, her gaze slanting down over the long, elegant length of him with loving, hungry eyes. She knew every inch of his magnificent body as intimately as she knew her own. She would have gambled her last penny that neither one of them could have walked into a room without the other being instantly aware of it. She waited for his head to turn, for those incredible dark eyes to meet hers, for his smile of delighted recognition. But she was wrong… Lucas wasn't aware of her at all…

She blindly allowed Spiro to lead her slowly through the crowd of guests; she had eyes for no one but Lucas. He was standing at the far end of the room with a group of three other people: his father, another elderly gentleman, and a young girl. He was smiling down at the girl with a look of such tenderness in his eyes that an inexplicable fear made Amber's blood run cold. His head was

slightly bowed, his shoulders curved in a protective attitude towards the girl, and Amber's heart froze in her
breast. She was vaguely aware of the long table they were
standing beside; for a second her eyes flickered to the centre point, a magnificent ice sculpture of a sailing ship.
Wildly whimsical, she wished she could get in it and sail
away, but inevitably her gaze was drawn back to the small
group. It was just a business deal, it had to be, she told
herself. She dimly felt Spiro squeeze her hand, and heard
through the roaring in her ears.

'I hate to say it, Amber, but I told you so...'

'Thanks.' She cast a furious sidelong glance at Spiro;
he was enjoying this. 'But it still does not mean you are
right. Lucas might not have had time to call me if, as you
say, he had a business meeting this afternoon.' She had to
hope; she could not face the alternative or it would destroy
her.

'If you believe that, you will believe anything. Where's
your pride, girl?' Spiro queried, raising one elegant brow,
but, sensing her distress, he added, 'Chin up, Amber.
Don't let the devil get you down.'

'He is not a devil,' she defended Lucas, but without her
usual conviction, and, glancing back at the group, she finally looked at the young girl at Lucas's side.

She was short and very Greek with an olive-skinned
complexion and long black hair tied back in a ponytail.
Pretty if a little plump. The dress she was wearing was a
concoction in pink satin with a gathered skirt, probably
ruinously expensive, but it did nothing for the girl's figure.
The girl was gazing up at Lucas, with a dreamy smile on
her face. One of her hands rested on his arm, and the other
was on his chest—there was no mistaking the intimacy of
the gesture.

'Is that child Christina Aristides?' Amber asked. 'The daughter you mentioned.'

'Yes.'

'Then you're wrong, Spiro. Lucas is no cradle-snatcher and that girl is young enough to be *his* daughter.' Her gaze strayed helplessly back to the dark head of her lover, and at that moment his head lifted, and his dark eyes clashed with Amber's.

She stared at the man she loved with all her heart, and she saw the coldness in his hard gaze as their glances locked. He did not even look surprised to see her. But she noticed his pupils dilate slightly, and the flare of desire in his eyes before he lowered his gaze, to sweep down over the shapely length of her and return blandly to her face.

Lucas Karadines shifted uncomfortably and shoved his hand in his trouser pocket. He had thought he had got himself under control enough to look at her again, but his body thought otherwise, much to his disgust. What the hell was she doing here with Spiro, anyway? He had told her to keep away from Spiro and she had deliberately defied him. But then that was Amber—she took a delight in challenging him on every level. A trait he could put up with in a girlfriend but not a trait a man wanted in a wife.

She looked stunning as always, her waist-length chestnut hair gleaming gold in the artificial light, the sleek black dress lovingly clinging to every curve of her magnificent body. Every man in the place was secretly eyeing her, he knew. She was sex personified, and his body had reacted instantly. He cursed under his breath. No man in his right mind would marry a girl like Amber, a girl who would have to be guarded every minute of every day from other predatory males. He smiled down at the young girl by his side. He had made the right decision; Christina would never cause him a moment's worry. Then he eyed Spiro again, and any guilt he was feeling at his own behaviour he transferred to Spiro. He might have guessed it was his damn nephew's entire fault. He had done it deliberately to embarrass him.

Amber watched Lucas shove his hand in his trouser pocket and knew he still wanted her. The beginnings of a smile curved her full lips as she waited for him to acknowledge her. But his desire was quickly replaced by anger as his dark eyes moved to narrow on her companion. The smile died from her lips before it was born as Lucas, with a dismissive arch of one dark brow, turned slightly and said something to his father, and then, smiling at his young companion, he took her hand in his and moved through the crowd, stopping as various people spoke to them.

Amber took the drink Spiro handed her and immediately took a long swallow; she needed something, anything. She was shaken to the core; she had never felt so utterly humiliated in her life. It was like being trapped in a nightmare, unable to move, or breathe. A frantic glance around the room, and she was amazed no one seemed to be aware of the enormity of what had just happened. Lucas had looked at her as if she was of no more interest to him than the dirt beneath his feet. It had to be a mistake, and for a wild moment she thought of flying over to him, and snatching his hand from the young girl.

'Any minute now, Amber, be cool,' Spiro murmured, his dark head bending towards her, shielding her face from view. 'Take a deep breath, don't let him see he has hurt you, don't give him the satisfaction.'

Hurt didn't begin to cover how she felt, and a slow-burning anger ignited in the pit of her stomach. She took a few deep, calming breaths, schooling her face into calm immobility.

'That's it,' Spiro said, and moved to her side just as Lucas and Christina stopped in front of them.

'Glad you could make it, Spiro, and you too, Amber,' Lucas said smoothly, and proceeded to introduce his companion. 'Allow me to introduce Christina Aristides. I have just acquired her father's business, and this evening is to celebrate the deal.'

Amber wanted to smash her fist in his face, scream and yell, demand to know why he had lied to her, but this was neither the time or the place. Instead she straightened her shoulders and pinned a smile on her face as she shook the young girl's hand. It wasn't the poor girl's fault, it was Lucas who was the swine.

Christina smiled demurely, and then, turning to Spiro, she punched him playfully on the arm. 'My, you are a dark horse, Spiro, you never mentioned that you were bringing your girlfriend with you tonight.' And then she added for Amber's benefit, 'I hope you did not mind me stealing your boyfriend for the afternoon, but Lucas was too tied up with business to go shopping with me.' The inference being Lucas was her boyfriend.

The tension between the other three was electric. Amber's eyes flew to Lucas's face—surely he would say something, deny it. She saw the cold anger in the depths of his eyes. He was furious she was here. Her presence had obviously upset his glittering celebration, or maybe for the first time in his life he actually felt embarrassed. But in a second Amber knew she was wrong. He stared back at her, his gaze chillingly remote. Amber had seen that look only once before when she'd tried to argue with him about Spiro—it had scared her then, but now it confirmed what she had probably known for the past twenty-four hours but refused to admit.

Shattered by his duplicity, she let her gaze trail over his

tall, muscular body. He was the sexiest man alive, but also
heartless. She finally saw him as the hard, ruthless Greek
tycoon that he had always been, but love had blinded her
to his real character. She tilted back her head, her golden
eyes challenging him, but he avoided her gaze, his whole
attention fixed on the young girl.

'Don't worry, Christina. I'm sure Amber didn't mind,'
Lucas said softly, and, turning to Spiro, he added, 'Though
I did not know you and Amber were still seeing each
other.'

'Oh, yes, Amber is not the sort to desert her friends, are
you, Amber, darling?' Spiro drawled pointedly, and, clasping an arm around her slender waist, he pulled her into
his side and pressed a swift kiss on her brow.

Amber let him—in fact she was glad of his support. Her
stomach churned and she wanted to be sick as the full
extent of Lucas's betrayal hit her. Her beautiful face lost
what little colour she had. How dared he introduce her to
Christina as though she were merely an acquaintance, a
friend of his nephew, instead of the woman who had
shared his bed for the best part of a year?

'So I see,' Lucas drawled mockingly. He knew Spiro
was gay.

His mockery was the last straw for Amber. Her wild
golden eyes clashed with Lucas's. 'I wonder, can anyone
say the same about you, Lucas? But, no, I seem to remember you telling me once you had no real friends. Perhaps because you only use people.' She saw his jaw
clench, a dark tide of colour surging up under his skin,
and a leap of fury in his eyes. Serves him right, Amber
thought.

'My, Lucas, a woman who does not admire you unre-
servedly, that must be a first,' Christina piped up.

'Amber is an old friend, and she and Spiro delight in

trying to needle me, it's just a joke.' Lucas smiled down at Christina, his voice softening. 'Nothing for you to worry about.'

Fury such as she had never known sent all the blood rushing back to Amber's head. Old friend! He had a nerve. The hand holding her glass of wine began to rise. Spiro, guessing her intentions, grasped her wrist.

'I am starving and I think you need a top up, Amber. Excuse us.' With his arm at her waist, he urged her away from the other couple. 'It would have been a futile gesture, Amber, throwing your drink over him—your glass is virtually empty,' he murmured, turning her back to the crowd to face the buffet table.

Amber was shaking, visibly shaking. She'd never felt such overwhelming rage in her life. 'I wasn't going to throw it over him,' she denied, turning blazing eyes up to Spiro's. 'I was going to screw the glass in his arrogant, lying face,' she confessed fiercely.

She was not a violent person, she had never harmed a living thing in her life, but for a second she had completely lost control. Suddenly she was appalled at her own actions, and her anger subsided. 'Thank you for stopping me, Spiro.' She tried to smile. 'Your better nature got the better of you—you said earlier you wanted me to cause a scene, and I thought you were joking. But the joke is on me and I've never felt less like laughing. I want to cry.'

'No, Amber. Tim was right and I was wrong.' His arm dropped from her waist and he lifted a hand to her chin and tilted her head up to face him. 'I should never have brought you here. I have to speak to my grandfather but then I am taking you straight home. Ten minutes at most, can you do it?'

A film of moisture hazed her glorious eyes, and she blinked furiously. 'I have to, I have no choice.' Imperceptibly she straightened her shoulders, her back ramrod straight as she fought for control, and won.

Spiro's hand fell from her chin, his dark eyes admiring her elegant form. 'You are the most beautiful, elegant lady in this room. You have more class in your little finger than the whole of this lot put together, and don't you forget it.'

Before Amber could respond old Mr Karadines interrupted them. He gave Spiro a hug and spoke to him in Greek, before turning to Amber.

'Amber, isn't it? Good to meet you again, and I'm glad to see you are still keeping this grandson of mine in order.'

'Hello, and I'm trying,' was as much as she could manage to say. A blessed numbness had enveloped her. She felt as if she were viewing the proceedings from outside her body—the pain was waiting for her, she knew, but her heart had not broken, it had simply solidified into a hard black stone in her breast.

'Good, good. I have been hearing great things about you from Clive here. Allow me to introduce you. Clive Thompson, my grandson's friend, Amber Jackson.'

Amber didn't have time to wonder why the old man had referred to her as Spiro's friend as the name of the tall, elegant blond-haired man registered, and she was holding out her hand to him. He was a top manager with Janson's merchant bank. He was only forty but already his reputation was legendary in the City.

She sensed rather than saw Lucas and Christina walk up and join the group, but she did not dare look. If she did she knew she would break down. Her hand was still held by Clive and she was grateful because it enabled her to find the strength not to tremble at Lucas's towering presence beside her.

'I have been longing to meet you as soon as Theo told me your name. Allow me to say you are as beautiful as you are brilliant, if not more so; a truly stunning combination.' His bright blue eyes smiled down into hers, and, lifting her fingers to his lips, he kissed the back of her hand before letting go.

'Oh, how gallant, Mr Thompson!' Christina's accented voice interrupted.

Amber glanced sideways and saw Lucas had moved closer to her with Christina clinging onto his other arm. Quickly she returned her attention to Clive, and saw his slightly raised eyebrows and brief polite smile at the young girl, before he returned his attention to Amber again and continued as if the other girl had not spoken.

'Brentford's are very lucky to have you, is the word in the City. Apparently you got your clients out of...' and he mentioned a high-tech company whose shares were on the way down and out '...even better than I did,' and he gave her an appreciative smile that Amber returned. They discussed the company in question in some detail. They were like-minded people.

'I was lucky,' she finally finished. Anything to do with business and she was not in the least intimidated. It was only in the love stakes she was a total idiot, it seemed.

'People make their own luck, Amber—I may call you Amber?' Clive grinned.

'Of course.' She heard what sounded like a grunt from Lucas, and felt the slight brush of his trouser-clad thigh against her hip.

Lucas did it deliberately. Inexplicably it angered him to hear Amber discussing business with the elegant Englishman, and he wanted to disconcert her, but she simply moved away. In that moment Lucas recognised the truth and his arm tightened around Christina. Amber did not need a man for anything other than sex and even that, as he knew to his cost, could be delayed because of her

work. He had never been in love but his idea of it was to
protect and care for his wife and family. Christina needed
his protection and in return he knew that as she was a
well-brought-up young Greek girl, her husband and children would always come first.

Amber felt as if she could feel Lucas breathing down
her neck and carefully moved closer to Spiro as Clive slid
one hand into the inside pocket of his jacket to withdraw
a gold-edged card. 'Here is my card—if you ever feel like
changing firms, I promise we will offer you a much better
package.'

A wry smile curved her full lips; she could not help it.
The ultimate irony. From her surprising lunch on Thursday
it had been like a roller-coaster ride of highs and lows,
finally to this, the worst night of her life, when it was
taking all her strength to simply keep standing, she was
being head-hunted by Janson's of all firms...

'And would your chairman, Sir David Janson, agree to
your proposition?' she prompted with an enviable touch
of cynicism, considering the tall, dark presence of Lucas
was within touching distance; the familiar scent of him
that filled her nostrils had her nerves at screaming-point.

'It would depend on the proposition, would it not,
Clive?' Lucas's deep voice queried sardonically.

'Oh, I'm sure Amber and I could work out a mutually
satisfactory arrangement.' Clive's blue eyes, gleaming
with very male appreciation, didn't leave Amber's as he
tagged on, 'And Sir Janson, of course.'

'I'm sure Amber does not want to talk business all night
with you men,' Christina inserted, smiling across at
Amber. 'I thought this was supposed to be a party.' Then
she added, 'Let's go find the rest room, and we can have
a gossip. I love your dress, and your necklace and earrings
are gorgeous; you must tell me where you got them.'

The bluntness with which Christina changed the subject stopped the conversation dead. Lucas's black eyes clashed with Amber's over the top of Christina's head, and she saw the warning glint in their depths, but she ignored it. Boldly she held his gaze, contempt blazing from her hazel eyes. For the first time that evening she felt in control.

'They were a birthday and Christmas present.' Amber smiled down at Christina. 'And, yes, I'll come with you,' she said, taking the young girl's arm. Let the swine sweat, let him wonder if she would tell his innocent *girlfriend* exactly who had given Amber the jewellery, she thought bitterly. Her rage was the only thing that kept her going as she walked out of the party and along the quiet hall to the powder room.

'Thank God we've escaped,' Christina groaned as they entered the powder room together, and, walking across to the row of vanity basins and dropping her purse on the marble top, she admired herself in the mirror above. 'An hour of my father and his friends and I feel like climbing the walls.' Turning to Amber, she added, 'You're lucky Spiro is young and doesn't take himself seriously. Lucas can be mind-bendingly boring, you've no idea.'

Shocked into silence, Amber watched the younger girl pull at the pink satin bodice of her dress. 'I ask you, Amber, would you be caught dead in a dress like this?'

'Well…' How to be diplomatic? Amber pondered. 'You must like it.' A high-pitched laugh greeted her comment.

'You're joking. I hate it, but then you are not Greek so you would not understand.'

Slowly Amber crossed to stand beside Christina. Her eyes met the other girl's in the mirror, and suddenly Christina seemed so much older and harder. 'Understand why you wear a dress you hate?' Amber prompted.

'Because my father expects me to look like his innocent

young daughter, and of course Lucas expects his fiancée to look like a shy young virgin, otherwise I would not be caught dead in pink satin.'

'Your fiancé!' Amber exclaimed, unable to disguise her horror.

'Yes, didn't Spiro tell you?' And, not waiting for an answer, Christina continued, 'Next weekend at our home in Athens my father is holding a huge party for my betrothal to Lucas and three weeks later we are getting married. He would have announced it tonight except it looks a bit too blatant even for a Greek to sign the business deal and sell your daughter in one afternoon.'

So it was all true. Amber's brain reeled under the shock. Spiro had not been exaggerating. She looked into the face of her rival and asked the question uppermost on her mind. 'Do you love Lucas?'

Christina laughed. 'No, but he loves me, or so he says, and it does not really matter anyway. I want to get married, the quicker the better.' Christina fiddled nervously with the clip of the small satin purse on the marble bench. 'Once I am married, I'm free. I get the money my mother left me, and, to give Lucas his due, he is renowned as a shrewd operator, so I have no doubt he will greatly increase the wealth of the family company. Therefore mine,' she said with some glee, and, finally noticing the look of shock and horror Amber could not hide, Christina laughed out loud. 'Don't look so shocked; it is a typical Greek arrangement.'

'But...but...' Amber spluttered '...you are so young.'

'I have just spent a year in a Swiss finishing-school, and those ski instructors are something else again. I'm not that young,' she offered with a very adult smile. 'Though I know what you mean—Lucas is a bit old. But Spiro did me a favour this afternoon. I think he was trying to warn me, but actually I was delighted when he told me Lucas apparently keeps a mistress, so I don't think he is going to be bothering me much in bed even when we are married.'

'You really don't mind?' Amber said slowly, the callousness of Christina's statement ringing in her ears. 'You don't care if your husband is unfaithful to you?'

'Not in the least, why should I with a fortune at my disposal?' And, picking up her purse, she opened it and withdrew some rolling tobacco. 'Do you want a smoke?'

Amber looked at the girl and the tobacco. 'No, I don't smoke.' Amber wondered why with her wealth she rolled her own.

'Pity.' Placing a hand on Amber's arm, Christina said, 'Don't look so surprised, and do me a favour, go out and tell Lucas I will be another five minutes. He does not know of my little vice.' She chuckled as she urged Amber towards the door.

Amber found herself out in the corridor without realising how she had got there.

'Where is Christina?' Lucas's deep voice demanded. Amber lifted her head, her stunned gaze meeting his dark brooding eyes. He was standing in the middle of the hall, his large body tense, waiting... But not for Amber...

'She said give her five minutes,' Amber stated bluntly. 'She also said you are her fiancé. How can that be, Lucas?' she hissed furiously. 'You live with me, it has to be a horrible mistake.'

'It is not a mistake.' The dark-lashed brilliance of his eyes clashed with hers; she was too upset to try and hide the hurt and anger in her own gaze. His expression hardened. 'I regret you had to find out this way. But then I had no knowledge of your continued association with my nephew or that he would bring you here tonight...'

Amber's mouth opened but no sound came out. The colossal arrogance of the man! Lucas was as good as saying it was Spiro's fault, that she had discovered his wicked betrayal.

'Look, Amber—' he laid a large hand on her arm, and furiously she brushed him off '—we have to talk.'

'A bit late for talk,' she snapped.

He straightened, squaring his broad shoulders. 'Keep your voice down,' he commanded, his dark eyes narrowing on her flushed, furious face. 'I will call tomorrow morning as arranged and explain.'

'My surprise,' she whispered, realising the full horrific extent of his betrayal. 'Christina was going to be my surprise!' Her voice rose an octave.

'Someone talking about me?' Christina came sauntering out of the cloakroom, her dark eyes almost feverishly bright, her smile brilliant.

Immediately Lucas curved a protective arm around Christina's shoulder, making it very clear where his loyalty lay. 'We were just discussing the engagement party next weekend. It was supposed to be a secret, you're very naughty.' He chided the young girl with such indulgence Amber felt sick.

Spiro sauntered up and slipped an arm around Amber's waist. 'What's all this? Plotting in corridors now.' He chuckled, and Amber clung to him like a life raft in a storm-tossed sea. Her knees were buckling and she thought she would faint; there was only so much hurt one body could stand and she was at the limit. Spiro, sensing her desperation, tightened his grip on her waist and listened as Christina, seemingly inexhaustible, went on at great length about the following weekend and extended an invitation to the party.

Finally when the young girl paused for breath Spiro

leapt in. 'Well, on behalf of both Amber and I, our heartiest congratulations to you, and we hope you both get the happiness you deserve!' he drawled sarcastically. 'Now, you will have to excuse us, but we have a prior engagement.' And within minutes Amber found herself out in the foyer of the hotel.

'I'm sorry, I am truly, truly sorry, Amber, I should never have brought you here.' But Amber wasn't listening. She'd been functioning on shock and adrenalin for the past hour, and now she was as spent as a burst balloon—she wanted to curl up and die.

'Take me home, Spiro.' And he did.

Sitting in the back seat of the cab, with Spiro's protective arm around her, Amber asked bleakly, 'Why, Spiro? You said your grandfather invited me. Why would he do that knowing Lucas and I...?' She broke off, to swallow the lump rising in her throat, her lashes wet with tears. 'How could he be so cruel?'

'You still don't see it,' Spiro said ruefully. 'I've avoided the subject for too long. I should have told you at the time, Amber, but it seemed a harmless enough deceit.' He glanced apologetically down at her tear-stained face. 'Remember the first time you saw Lucas, when he arrived at my party madder than hell? Well, it was because he had just discovered I was taking Tim to our villa in Greece for the Easter holiday and I was about to confess to Grandfather that I was gay. Lucas tried to talk me out of it, saying it would kill the old man if he thought his only grandson was gay. Which is why he asked you out to dinner, and asked you to accompany Tim and I on holiday. Lucas is not above using anybody to protect the old man. Consequently, he subtly let Grandfather know you and Tim were like brother and sister. But you and I had a much closer relationship; after all, you had been living in my house for four years. Lucas can be very convincing, as you know.'

'You mean all this time your grandfather has thought you and I are a couple? But that's impossible...' But was it? she asked herself. Lucas had made no approach to her until they had returned to England, and she had never met his father again until tonight.

Then she remembered their very first dinner date. When Lucas had invited her to the villa, he had also asked her to do him a favour. He knew she was close to Tim and Spiro, and he had asked her to use her influence on the pair to tone down their behaviour in front of his father when they were all at the villa. The old man was rather old-fashioned that way. Of course, Amber had said yes.

Now it all made a horrible kind of sense. Lucas would do anything for his father, including marrying a suitable rich little Greek girl. Spiro was right...

'Think about it, Amber. Has Lucas ever taken you anywhere in public where Grandfather was likely to hear about it? No. While you thought you were building a relationship, a home, with a thoroughly modern man, Lucas had no such intentions.'

Amber's face was bleak, her mouth bitter and twisted as the full import of Spiro's revelation sank in. She tried to speak and found herself shivering compulsively. She could not believe she had been so blind, so stupid...

CHAPTER THREE

AMBER knew once she let the first tear fall that she would never be able to stop. Kicking off her shoes, she locked the door and padded across the polished wood floor to the spiral staircase. Grasping the rail, she ascended to the galleried sleeping area like an old woman. Spiro had asked her to go back to his place, but she'd refused. He had done enough for her for one night, she thought bitterly.

Stripping off her clothes, she walked into the huge bathroom. She glanced at the circular white marble Jacuzzi sunk into the floor, and quickly away as too many memories flooded back. Skirting the bath, she stepped into the double shower. She turned the tap on full, and stood under the power jets and let the water pound her slender body. She closed her eyes, but she could not block out the image of Lucas naked on his knees in the shower with her. Soaping every inch of her tender flesh from the tips of her toes to her head in what she had thought was complete adoration.

Why? Why had Lucas done this to her? her mind screamed, and the iron control she had exerted over her emotions all evening finally broke. The tears slowly squeezed from her eyes to slide down her cheeks. The trickle became a flood as she wept out her pain and grief, the tears mingling with the powerful spray until Amber fell to her knees, her arms wrapped around her middle, her head bowed, completely broken, defeated...

Her body shivering, Amber slowly opened her eyes. She was huddled on the floor of the shower. When had the hot water run out and turned to icy cold? She had no idea. She was freezing, her limbs numb. Slowly she staggered to her feet, turned off the tap and stepped out of the shower. Pulling a large bath towel from the rail, she wrapped it toga-style around her shaking body. She caught sight of her reflection in the mirror above the vanity basin—her eyes were red-rimmed and puffy, her skin pale and cold as death.

She was still wearing the emerald necklace and earrings. Carefully she removed both, and, walking out of the bathroom, she dropped them on the dressing table, then pulled out the seat and sat down. Picking up the hair-dryer, she switched it on and methodically began drying her long hair.

Lucas had loved to see her naked with her hair smoothed silkily over her breasts. Her eyes filled with moisture at the memory, and, leaping to her feet, she staggered across the room and flung herself down on the bed. She turned her face into the pillow, shaken by another violent storm of weeping.

When it was over she felt curiously calm, and as it was just dawn she got to her feet and began to dress. She did not bother with a bra, she had no need for one, but slipped into skimpy white lace briefs. She withdrew grey- and blue-checked trousers from the wardrobe and a V-neck button-through matching blue cashmere cardigan, and put them on. She slipped her feet into soft leather loafers and descended the spiral staircase. She crossed the vast expanse of the living area to the kitchen, and opened the door just as the first rays of sun shone though the window.

Amber switched on the kettle, made herself a cup of instant coffee, and, taking it back with her into the living room, she sat down on one of the soft-cushioned sofas. She picked up the remote control for the television and

switched it on. It was the twenty-four-hour news channel.
She watched and waited...

Amber heard the key turn in the lock, and, switching off
the television, she stood up and slowly turned to face the
door.

To the man entering the room, she looked cool, calm
and collected, and beautiful. 'Amber, I am glad you are
here. I thought you might have gone back with Spiro after
last night,' Lucas said smoothly, closing the door behind
him and striding towards her.

Amber watched him approach. He was casually dressed
in faded denim jeans, a cream-coloured roll-neck sweater
and tan leather jacket. His black hair was windswept; he
had never looked more attractive to her, or more out of
her reach.

Her heart hardened against his masculine appeal. 'Why
would I do that, Lucas? This is my home,' she queried
coolly. A bone-numbing anger had replaced her earlier
grief.

'Good, I hoped you would be sensible.' His long legs
slightly splayed, he stopped about a foot away from her,
his dark eyes sweeping over her long hair falling loose to
her waist, and back up, lingering for a second too long on
the proud thrust of her breasts against the soft cashmere
sweater.

Amber saw his pupils darken, and the sudden tension
in his broad frame. He was not immune to her, that much
was obvious, and it simply fuelled her anger. 'Sensible is
not the word I would have chosen,' she declared bitterly.
'I don't feel in the least sensible after last night, I feel
madder than hell, and demand an explanation. I thought
you were my boyfriend, my partner. We live together, for

God's sake!' she cried, aware of the consuming bile rising in her throat as she studied his hard features.

Abruptly Lucas stepped back a pace, and she had the satisfaction of seeing his face darken with suppressed anger, or was it embarrassment? He didn't appreciate being called to account for his behaviour. 'I agree,' he said curtly. 'And I apologise—last night should never have happened. Christina should not have told you we were getting engaged next weekend. But then you should not have been at the party. You have Spiro to thank for last night's fiasco, not I.'

'Oh, no, you can't blame this on Spiro, you lying swine,' she shot back furiously. 'You told me you could not get back from New York until Saturday—pressure of work, you said. What a joke!' Blazing golden eyes clashed with his and what she saw in their obsidian depths sent an icy shiver down her spine.

'I did not lie. I said I could not *meet* you until Saturday, which was perfectly true. I had a prior engagement for Friday evening,' he drawled cynically.

'An engagement for the rest of your life, if Christina is to be believed. I have never been so embarrassed or humiliated in all my life, and I want to know *why*? You owe me that much,' Amber demanded, her voice rising stridently.

Lucas stepped forward and closed a powerful hand over both of hers. 'Calm down and listen to me,' he snapped back, his black eyes hard on her lovely face. 'I had no desire to embarrass or hurt you in any way. I had every intention of telling you our affair was over before announcing my betrothal. I have never in my life begun a sexual relationship with a woman without first divesting myself of her predecessor. It is a rule of mine.'

'Bully for you!' she snorted inelegantly, but just the

touch of his hand on hers made her pulse race and she despised herself for it. 'You are so moral,' she managed to drawl sarcastically. 'Is that supposed to make me feel better that you are dumping me?'

'Dumping...' a grimace of distaste tightened his hard mouth '...is not how I would have put it. Our affair has reached its conclusion, and I hope we can part friends.'

This is not happening to me, this cannot be happening to me, Amber told herself over and over again. The blind, arrogant conceit of the man was unbelievable. *Friends*—he wanted them to be *friends*... Didn't he know he had broken her heart, destroyed her dreams, her life? She looked up and saw the flicker of impatience in his dark eyes, the aloof expression on his handsome face, and she had her answer. It was obvious he was wondering how to extricate himself as quickly as possible.

'And what about me?' Amber asked quietly, amazed that her voice didn't break.

'Amber, we have had some great times together, but now it is over, it has to be. I have reached the age—' he walked away from her, pacing the length of the room '—when it is time for me to settle down. I want a wife, a family, a home, and Christina is going to give me all that.' Then, spinning on his heel, he walked slowly back towards her.

'You're bright and ambitious, I know you have a brilliant future ahead of you. But, for me, Christina is the answer. You understand.'

The numbness that had protected her for the past few hours vanished. He was ripping her heart to shreds with every word he spoke. 'No, no, I don't.' She raised her eyes to meet his. 'I thought we were a couple, and that this was our home.' Even as she said the words, she saw the gleam of cynical amusement in his dark eyes as he glanced around the room and back at Amber.

'Oh, come on, Amber, don't play the innocent, it does not suit you. This was never meant to be a home, a living area with an open-galleried bedroom and a sybaritic bathroom. Could you see me entertaining my family and friends in this place?' One dark brow arched sardonically. 'I think not...'

Amber exploded; her hand swung in a wide arc and smashed across his face. 'I should have done that last night,' she yelled. 'You arrogant, conceited, two-timing bastard.'

Lucas raised a hand to his cheek, and rubbed where she had hit him. 'Perhaps I deserved that, so I'll let you get away with it, Amber, but only once,' he declared grimly. 'Accept it is over between us and move on. I have.'

She watched the dark stain appear on his cheek where she had hit him, and immediately regretted her action. Involuntarily she raised her hand, intending to stroke the side of his face, but her wrist was caught in an iron grip. 'No.'

She moved forward and lifted her other hand to rest on the soft wool sweater covering his broad chest. 'I'm sorry,' she murmured. But the familiar feel of his hard muscles beneath her fingers sent shivers of delight arcing though her body. She loved this man with all her heart, and helplessly she tilted back her head and looked up into his darkly attractive face. 'Please, Lucas.' She felt him stiffen, and she moved even closer, and slid her hand up over his chest and around the nape of his neck.

'We are so good together, Lucas, you know we are.' It had been two long months since she had felt the warmth of his caress and she ached for him. Suddenly she was fighting for her man, and using every skill at her disposal. She saw his pupils dilate as her breasts brushed against his hard chest, and involuntarily her fingers trailed with tactile delight up through the hair at the back of his neck. 'Kiss me, Lucas, you know you want to.' Gently she urged his head down towards her eager lips.

'No, Amber.' His large hands gripped her shoulders to push her away just as she brushed her lips against his, the tip of her tongue darting out to gain access to his mouth. She heard the intake of his breath as his arms jerked her to him and their bodies met in searing contact, and she was lost in the dark, heady hunger of the kiss for an instant, before his hands caught her shoulders and he forced her back at arm's length.

Lucas Karadines didn't like the way she affected him. His dark eyes glittered dangerously. His own mother had been addicted to sex, one lover after another until she'd died. Her last lover had kicked a young boy of thirteen out on the street. So he fought the temptation and won. 'You are a very sexy lady, Amber, but I am not such a bastard as to take what you're offering. It's over.'

'But if you want a wife, why not me? I love you, Lucas, and I thought you loved me,' Amber pleaded, raising an unsteady hand and tenderly brushing a few black silky strands of his hair from his brow. 'I could give you children, anything you want.' She was laying her heart, her life, on the line, begging him. She had lost all pride, all anger, and she didn't care. She looked deep into his dark eyes, her own beseeching his. She thought she saw a flicker of uncertainty in the depths of his, but she was mistaken.

'No, Amber.' A grim smile twisted the corners of his sensual mouth. 'I never lied to you—I never once mentioned love.'

His words lashed her like a whip flailing her alive; she closed her eyes for an instant, searching her mind. He was right, he had never said he loved her. How had she made such an enormous mistake? His hands fell from her shoulders and she opened her eyes. She could actually see him mentally withdrawing from her as he physically moved back a step.

'You are a lovely girl, but you are not the wife and mother type.' His breathing was heavy but his dark eyes held unmistakable, unyielding, will-power. 'You're a career woman—you compete in a male-dominated industry, and you are as good as, if not better than, most of the men, by all accounts. You wouldn't last six months as a stay-at-home wife. You would be bored out of your skull. So don't fool yourself, Amber. You're strictly lover material.'

She listened with growing horror. 'Is that really what you think?' she muttered sickly. 'All this time you saw me as your lover, a sex object, nothing else.'

He shrugged his broad shoulders. 'The term is not important. What we shared was a mutually agreeable relationship.' His dark eyes skimmed over her shapely figure and he made no effort to hide his masculine appreciation. 'And great sex.'

His deliberate sensual scrutiny made her breasts swell in instant awareness, and hot colour flooded her cheeks and he noticed. 'Be honest, Amber, you're no shy young maid, never were. You're a born hedonist, you thrive on sensual pleasure, the pleasure I gave you. But you're a sophisticated lady—admit it, if we have spent six months together since we met it would be a miracle, and that mostly in bed. Ours was a sexual relationship, nothing more.'

For him maybe, but for Amber it had been everything. She only had to look at him to remember the powerful strength of his all-male body when he possessed her, caressed her. 'Nothing more,' she parroted his words with horror.

'Exactly.' He sounded relieved, actually believing she had agreed with him. And blithely carried on adding insult to injury. 'But Christina is different. She is sweet and innocent and has no desire to do anything other than be my wife, and bear my children.'

Her teeth had bitten into her bottom lip as she listened to him praise his Christina, and the salty tang of blood coated her tongue. 'I was innocent until you seduced me,' she reminded him, the hurt almost too much to bear. He knew she'd been a virgin when he'd first made love to her. She had given him the greatest gift a woman could give a man, her heart, body and soul, and he had the gall to label her a hedonist...

'Ah, Amber...' He shook his dark head in a mocking gesture. 'You know as well as I do that it was no great moral conviction that kept you a virgin. It was probably the fact you had spent the last four years living with a couple of gay men and their friends and hadn't much opportunity. You would have jumped into bed with me the first day you arrived at the villa.' Lucas shot her a cynical smile. 'With your minuscule bikinis, and designer clothes, you were no retiring violet. You were desperate for a man, and it was my restraint, my strict rule not to take on a new lover without first leaving the old that meant we waited until I had got back from New York. Seduction did not come into it.'

'I see.' And she did... She closed her eyes for a brief moment, blocking out the picture of his hard, cynical face, her hands clenching into fists at her sides. He thought of her as a sexy woman who had been easy to take, who could respond to any man's caress with equal fervour, not just his. Eagerly she had followed where he'd led, plunging the erotic depths with a hunger that had known no bounds, confident that he'd loved her, and everything had been permissible between two lovers. Her own innate honesty forced her to admit it was not all his fault. She had deliberately set out to appear to be the sort of woman she'd imagined he wanted. 'Hoist by her own petard' was the phrase that sprang to mind... Lucas did not know her at all, never had, and, worse, did not want to.

'Tell me, Lucas, if I had held out for a ring, would you have married me?' Amber demanded, black anger filling her heart at his chauvinistic attitude, never mind his betrayal.

He stared at her, his hard mouth suddenly cruel. 'With you the question would never arise. If you remember, I did ask you to give up work so we could spend more time together, and you could not even do that. So the answer is no. You're a thoroughly modern woman, equal to a man, you work hard and play hard.'

'And your Christina is not?' She arched one delicate brow in a gesture of mocking disbelief. 'A year in Switzerland, all those hunky ski instructors,' she taunted him, the memory of the young girl's conversation last night still clear in her mind.

That appeared to catch him on the raw, and for a moment he looked almost savage. 'Leave Christina out of this,' he ordered curtly. ' You disappoint me, Amber, I did not think you could sink so low as to maliciously malign a young girl's reputation, a girl you hardly know,' he drawled contemptuously.

Amber stared at his hard, cold face, willing herself not to feel hurt by his immediate defence of the girl. Then it hit her. 'You've never slept with Christina, and you think you love her. I'm right, aren't I?' she demanded, not sure whether to laugh or cry. Lucas Karadines, a powerful, dynamic businessman viewed with fear and awe by his competitors, was fooled by a pseudo-innocent eighteen-year-old going on eighty.

'Yes, I love Christina, and I am going to marry her.' He gave the only answer he could. He wasn't sure he believed in love. His mother had fallen in *love* with depressing regularity, when basically it had been sex. He had no intention of making the same mistake. He had chosen carefully and made the commitment to Christina and both of their families in traditional Greek fashion, and he was determined to honour it and make his marriage a success.

Amber stared at him. Oh, heavens, she silently screamed. It was true. She saw the absolute sincerity in his dark eyes, heard it in the tone of his voice, and was convinced. Never mind business, Lucas honestly thought he loved the girl. Her shoulders drooping, she closed her eyes for a second, all the fight draining out of her, and a dull acceptance taking its place. 'I suppose I'd better go and pack.'

'No.' Lucas caught her shoulder and turned her back to face him. 'Sit down, Amber. I am not so unfeeling I would see you deprived of your home.'

It never was a home, he had made that abundantly clear, but her traitorous limbs gave way beneath her and she sank thankfully down onto the soft cushions. 'No.' Amber looked at him towering over her, with all the bitterness of her feelings in her eyes. 'Then what now, Lucas? If you're waiting for my blessing, you're wasting your time.' He was sliding something from the inside pocket of his jacket—a long manila envelope.

'You have no need to leave—I am going. I'll send someone round this afternoon to collect the few things I have here, and you'd better keep these—you will need them.'

The last half-hour had been the hardest of Lucas Karadines's life. It had taken all his monumental control not to take what Amber had been offering. He would not dare come back himself, because deep down he knew he would not be able to resist making love to her one more time. He dropped the envelope and his set of keys to the apartment down onto the sofa beside her. 'Goodbye, Amber.' He hesitated for a second, his night-black eyes lingering on her pale face. 'I'm...'

'Just go.' Her lips twisted; if he said sorry she would kill him. His dark head bent towards her and she felt the brush of his lips against her hair and flinched. She didn't need his pity. And, flinging her head back, she sat rigidly on the edge of the sofa, her golden eyes hating him.

Lucas straightened up. 'Look after yourself.' And, brushing past her, he headed for the door. He opened the door and paused, finally turning to add, 'By the way, if you're thinking of taking up the offer Clive Thompson made you, don't. The man is not to be trusted.'

A harsh laugh escaped her. 'It takes one to know one. Get out.' And, picking up a scatter cushion, she flung it at him. It bounced harmlessly off the closed door and fell to the floor.

Amber looked around her at the apartment that she had mistakenly thought was a home with new eyes, and groaned out loud. Lucas was right. How could she have been so stupid, so gullible? She had tried to add a few touches, the scatter cushions, a couple of framed photographs of her mother, and Tim. A painting she had bought on a trip around a gallery with Spiro. The rug was the only thing in the place that she and Lucas had chosen together. It was exactly as Lucas had said: a bachelor pad, or a love-nest.

She had to get out, she thought brutally. It didn't matter

where as long it was somewhere that did not remind her of Lucas. But first she had to pack up his clothes—hadn't he said he was sending someone over to collect them?

She jumped to her feet and the manila envelope fell from her knee to the floor; she bent down and picked it up. Slitting open the envelope, she withdrew a folded document. She read it, her eyes widening in amazement that quickly turned to fury. Her first thought was to rip it up, but she hesitated... The paper dropped from her hand to flutter back to the floor.

It was the deeds for the apartment in her name, and it was dated two weeks ago. She felt sick and defiled; he had paid her off like some cheap whore. Perhaps not cheap, she amended, but her fury knew no bounds. She marched into the kitchen and took the scissors from the kitchen drawer, and then headed straight upstairs. With grim determination she slid back the wardrobe door. Earlier she had run her hands over Lucas's clothes, in need of reassurance. Now she touched them for a completely different reason.

Working quickly, Amber emptied the wardrobe and drawers of every item that belonged to Lucas, and packed them in one suitcase. That told her something. Her mouth tightened in a rare grimace of cynicism. If she had needed any further convincing that Lucas had considered her nothing more than a convenient bed partner, the fact that he had left so few clothes in the place she had thought was his home said it all.

When a little man called a few hours later and asked for Mr Karadines's luggage she handed over the suitcase without a word, and closed the door in the man's face. She only wished she could close the door to her heart as firmly on the memory of Lucas Karadines.

* * *

A few hours later on the other side of London, Lucas Karadines stood in the middle of his hotel bedroom and stared in fury at the pair of trousers his father's valet was holding out to him.

'I'm afraid, sir, I've checked, and all three suits in the luggage I collected from the lady's apartment are the same.' The little wizened man was having the greatest difficulty keeping the smile from his face. 'The fly panel has been rather roughly cut out of all of them.'

A torrent of Greek curses turned the air blue as Lucas stormed across the room and picked up the telephone and began pressing out the number he knew by heart. Then suddenly he stopped halfway through, and replaced the receiver. No, there was no point—Amber was out of his life and he wanted it to stay that way. But a reluctant smile quirked the corners of his firm mouth. He should have expected some such thing. Amber was a passionate character in every way; it was what had drawn him to her in the first place. A shadow darkened his tanned features as he instructed the valet to press another suit. With brutal honesty he recognised Amber had some justification. She should never have discovered by a third party their relationship was over, and certainly not in so public a manner.

CHAPTER FOUR

CARRYING her mug of coffee, Amber made her way to the kitchen. Draining the last dregs, she rinsed the cup in the sink, and dried it with the tea towel.

It was little more than a week since Lucas had told her he was marrying Christina and walked out of her life. She had gone to work as usual, and she had waited. Waited and hoped for a miracle—for Lucas to change his mind. But by Wednesday she had bowed to the inevitable and set the wheels in motion to move out of the apartment. And if in the deepest corner of her heart hope lingered, she ignored it.

When Spiro had called her Sunday afternoon from Athens, confirming that the engagement party of Lucas Karadines and Christina Aristides the previous evening had been a great success, it was simply the final nail in the coffin that held all her dreams.

If she needed any more confirmation, she only had to look at this morning's newspaper lying on the kitchen bench open at the gossip page. A picture of the couple was prominently displayed. She crushed up the paper and wrapped the coffee mug in it. Then she carefully placed it on the top of the rest of the kitchen implements already packed in the large tea chest that sat in the middle of the kitchen floor. Finished...

She had applied on Friday to have today, Monday, off work, because realistically she'd known she would be moving out. Everything was packed, the For Sale sign had been erected an hour earlier by the carpenter employed by the estate agent she had consulted to dispose of the apartment. She could not live in it, and the proceeds would help some charity. She did not care any more.

Since the night at the London hotel, and the sleepless nights since, she had gone beyond feeling pain into a state of complete detachment. It was not completely Lucas's fault. She should have remembered 'To thine own self be true.' She had transformed herself virtually overnight into a sophisticated lady in her determination to win Lucas, and that was how he had seen her. She had never let him see the naive young country girl she had been, who just happened to have a gift for figures. Now it was too late. He had fallen in love with someone else, and she would never be that girl again anyway.

On Saturday she'd made a start on getting her life back. She had rented a small cottage with a garden in the village of Flamstead, within manageable commuting distance of the City. Amber recognised she had loved unwisely and too much, but she had silently vowed no man would ever be able to hurt her like that again.

Amber walked back into the living room, and glanced at the gold watch on her wrist. The removal firm was due to arrive at three. Another two hours to kill.

The telephone was still connected: she could call Tim, but she had no desire to talk to him or Spiro for that matter. She was still mad at Spiro's revelation yesterday that, at the engagement party, for a joke he had hinted to his grandfather and Lucas that his engagement to Amber might be next. Spiro was a wickedly mischievous devil—he could not help himself.

She heard the knock on the front door and sighed with relief. Good, the removal men were early, almost unheard of in London. Walking over to the door, she opened it, the beginnings of a smile curving her generous mouth. At last something was going her way. Her smile vanished, her mouth falling open in shock as she found herself staring into the hard black eyes of Lucas Karadines.

Her first instinct was to slam the door in his face but he anticipated her action by brushing past her and into the centre of the room.

Mechanically, she closed the door behind him. 'What do you want?' she demanded, her mind spinning, fighting to control the tremor in her voice and the swift surge of hope his appearance aroused in her. On a completely feminine note Amber wished she were wearing something better than a battered old cotton shirt and a pair of scruffy black leggings from her student days.

Spinning around to face her, Lucas regarded her silently for what seemed an interminable length of time, but Amber quickly gathered from the harsh expression on his dark, slightly saturnine features that he had certainly not sought her out for reconciliation.

'I said, what do you want?' she repeated coolly. He looked dynamic and infinitely masculine, his casual jeans and heavy wool sweater barely detracting from the raw vitality of the man. His eyes didn't leave hers for a second, and she began to feel a rising tide of bitter resentment as the blood raced through her veins in the old familiar way.

'I want to study what a woman scorned really looks like,' Lucas stated with studied indolence, his eyes raking over her from the top of her head, over her face, her hair hanging loose about her shoulders, down over the firm thrust of her breasts clearly outlined against the fine cotton, then lower to her slim hips and long legs perfectly moulded by the black leggings. His narrowed gaze rested on her bare feet, then back to her face.

'I ignored the destruction of a few suits,' he drawled silkily, taking a step towards her.

She swallowed painfully, colour flooding her cheeks. She'd forgotten about her futile attempt at revenge: the mangled suits, and all the gifts he had ever given her flung on top. But it was as nothing to what he had done to her. Her head lifted fractionally. Pride uppermost. 'You can afford it,' she snapped.

One eyebrow lifted slightly. 'A bagatelle, I grant you, compared to the price of this apartment. I see you have wasted no time in trying to sell it,' he opined silkily and moved closer. 'I ignored the insult intended by the return of the presents I gave you.' And, catching hold of her hand, he drew her towards him, despite the struggle she made to break free. His glance spearing her ruthlessly, he added, 'But I will never allow you to marry Spiro simply so he can get his hands on his inheritance before he is of age. I'll see you in hell first.'

The statement was quiet and deadly, and Amber suddenly realised his temper was held in check by a tenuous thread. 'Let go of me,' she demanded, her own anger rising. as she tried to escape his steel-like grasp.

'I will when I have your promise you will stay away from Spiro.'

She almost laughed out loud. Lucas actually thought Spiro had been serious when he had voiced the prospect of marrying her to his grandfather. But she saw no reason to make it easy for Lucas. How dared he come here and threaten her?

'I can live with who I like and I can marry who I like, and it has damn all to do with you. In case you have forgotten, you are engaged to be married. In fact, I am amazed you could tear yourself away from the arms of your fiancée so quickly after your betrothal. Not as passionate as you hoped, hmm?' she prompted. 'Now, let go of my arm and get lost.' And with a fierce tug she freed her wrist from his grasp and swiftly stepped around him, heading for the stairs.

With an angry oath he spun around and caught the back of her shirt, bringing her to an abrupt halt. She strained forwards and he tugged harder so she fell back against him, the buttons popping off her shirt at the rough treatment. She tried to elbow him in the stomach. But he quickly turned her around and held her hard against the long length of his impressive frame. She began to struggle in earnest, striking out at him with her fists, making little impression on the broad, muscular wall of his chest.

'Let go of me, you great brute.' Her temper finally exploded. 'I know your game. Not content with marrying a poor kid half your age for her father's business, you're so bloody greedy that you're terrified Spiro will manage to get his hands on his half of the business. God, you make me sick!' she told him furiously.

Her wrists were caught and held together with effortless ease behind her in one large hand, his dark eyes leaping with rage as they burned into hers. 'You foul-mouthed little bitch! You would marry a man you know is gay simply to get back at me.'

'Don't flatter yourself,' she jeered. 'I don't give a toss about you.'

'But you enjoyed what I could give you,' he said harshly as though he wasn't really making a statement but remembering. 'Something Spiro is not capable of.'

If Amber had not known better, she might have thought he was jealous on a personal level, but she knew he was only worried about retaining complete control of the company. Once Spiro came of age, heaven knew what he would do with his share. He was a loose cannon in the business sense, her own intelligence told her that. But it was still no reason for Lucas to try and bully her.

'How would you know what Spiro is capable of?' she taunted him. 'He could be bisexual. But it does not really matter because Spiro is a friend, and with you for an uncle he needs all the friends he can get,' she opined scathingly.

'And of course you have no ulterior motive in befriending Spiro,' Lucas drawled cynically. 'What did my nephew promise you for marrying him—a percentage of his inheritance, or is it pure, old-fashioned revenge you're after?'

He towered over her, dwarfing her not inconsiderable height. Suddenly she became aware of the hard heat of his body. His aroused body! Her eyes clashed with his, and his darkened as the chemistry between them renewed itself with frightening force.

'Certainly not his body, we both know that is not his scene,' Lucas drawled huskily, his dark gaze moving down to the luscious outline of her lips.

Amber could not help it. She regarded him hungrily, his harshly etched features as familiar to her as her own. She lowered her eyes in case he might see the need, the hunger flooding through her, and suddenly she became aware that in the struggle her shirt had come open almost to her waist. One firm breast was completely exposed, the other only partially covered. But she was not alone in her discovery; Lucas's sharply indrawn breath and something in his eyes that had always warned her in the past of his stirring hunger for sex made her tremble. His free hand slid cool fingers down her flushed cheeks, circling the outline of her full mouth.

Amber realised she should be fighting him, but could only gaze at him mesmerised as his hand captured the gentle curve of her nape, and electric tension filled the air.

'*Christos!* But you probably could turn Spiro!' He laughed harshly. 'You are sinfully sexy.' His gaze swept down to her bare breasts, and her nipples peaked in telling arousal; she was incapable of hiding her response to him. In that second Lucas knew he should never have come back here—she was utterly irresistible.

Speechless, Amber remained pinned against him, her pulse racing wildly out of control, and suddenly she realised with blinding clarity she did not want to hide her response. The musky scent of masculine arousal teased her nostrils, and, as she felt the muscles of his powerful thighs pressing against her, she tilted back her head and saw his eyes were all black pupil, his desire a primitive need as great as her own. Involuntarily her back arched ever so slightly, lifting her breasts to greater prominence.

She heard his guttural curse a moment before his mouth found hers, kissing her with a bruising, demanding hunger, grinding her lips back against her teeth. A wild, basic recklessness filled her, and she responded with a fiery fervour, her mouth opening to his. She forgot he was engaged to another. She forgot he had betrayed her. There was only the moment...

He kissed her with a searing passion, and she shuddered, responding to his passion, matching it with her own. The kiss they exchanged was primitive and out of control. Every bit of Amber burned with a need, a hunger that was almost pain, and when he trailed sharp, biting kisses down her throat and finally closed his teeth over one pouting nipple she whimpered, but not with pain.

Her hands were set free, and instead of pushing him away she gloried in her freedom to touch him. Her hands worked frenziedly beneath his sweater. Lucas helped her by lifting his head and tearing his sweater off, before hauling her back against him. Her fingers traced over the breadth of his chest, finding the hard male nipples in the silky mat of hair and doing some tantalising of her own.

It had been months and she hadn't realised how needy she had been.

Lucas lifted her high in his arms and laid her down on the hardwood floor in one smooth motion. 'Damn you, Amber,' he growled, following her down, his chiselled features dark with passion.

His words hurt and angered her, but nothing could stop the storm of desire sweeping through her. He removed her leggings and briefs with enviable ease, while Amber fumbled with the belt of his trousers; quickly he guided her hands and in a second he was almost naked.

She heard the sharp intake of his breath as her fingers slid along his thigh and his mouth ground down on hers with furious greed. Their bodies met with a searing impact that made her shudder with pleasure.

Lucas lifted his head, his black eyes sweeping almost violently over her naked body. His head bent and he suckled the hard, aching peak of her breast as swiftly he parted her legs. Every other time he had enjoyed making love to her long and slow, teasing and tantalizing, drawing out the experience for ages. But this time it was like a dam bursting, sweeping everything before it, as without hesitating he positioned himself between her slender thighs and joined them fiercely together.

Amber gasped and writhed, half mad with wanting him, the hardness of the floor, the anger not love that fuelled the joining—none of it mattered. It was enough he was here with her—in her—and if it was to be the last time, she didn't care. He wanted her.

Hot and breathless bodies wet with sweat, they moved together in a mind-blowing, consuming passion. The climax when it came was a shuddering ecstatic release that lifted Amber to another universe, where her mind closed down, and the body was everything. The ecstatic shivers went on and on long after Lucas lay heavily on top of her, the rasping sound of his breathing the most wonderful music to Amber's ears.

She refused to believe he could behave like this with her and yet love someone else, and when he moved to roll off her she followed him around. Sprawled across his wide chest, still joined, she looked into his darkly flushed handsome face, but his eyes were closed.

'Lucas,' she tenderly murmured his name, and, reaching up, she brushed the sweat-slicked hair from his brow. Slowly his eyes opened and he looked at her with such contempt she almost cried out.

'Amber,' he grated, mockingly brushing her off him as if he were swatting a fly and jumping to his feet, as though he could not get away from her quickly enough.

She lay where he had left her and watched him. He had not removed his shoes, and he should have looked stupid with his trousers around his ankles, but he didn't. She let her eyes stray over every perfect inch of his bronzed body, committing every curve and muscle, pore and hair to memory, because she instinctively knew this was the very last time she would ever see him this way.

His dark eyes wandered insolently over her as he pulled up his trousers. The taut line of his mouth gave way to a thin, cruel smile. '*Christos.*' He laughed harshly, and slipped his sweater over his head. Adjusting the sleeves, he added, 'I was right about you—as sexy as sin and far too seductive to wed.'

Lucas knew he was being cruel, but it was a pure defence mechanism. He could not believe what he had just done! He had lost control completely, and he hated himself for it. He was strongly puritanical when it came to women, totally monogamous for as long as the relationship lasted, and he had every intention of being totally faithful to his wife. Hell! He almost groaned out loud. Betrothed three days to Christina, and already…

'You're no saint,' Amber's voice cut into his tortured thoughts.

His black eyes roamed over her lovely face, her cheeks burning with angry colour. She was exquisite, and briefly he closed his eyes, a deep black pit opening up before him, his supreme self-confidence shaken to its core as for a moment he doubted his decision to marry Christina. He opened his eyes. It was too late now. He was Greek, first and foremost, he was engaged to a Greek girl, his father was delighted, Christina's father was ecstatic. He had made the right decision. It was simply he had been celibate for too long, he told himself, and *almost* believed it…

'So much for your moral code, off with the old before the new,' Amber declared fiercely, breaking the tension-filled silence, and, sitting up, she pulled the shirt that was hanging off her back around her chest.

He smiled down at her mockingly, forcing himself not to weaken. 'Oh, for heaven's sake, get dressed.' If she didn't he was in grave danger of falling down on top of her again, eyeing her flustered attempt to pull her shirt around the luscious curve of her breasts. Shame and guilt made him add, 'You disgust me. I disgust myself.'

Amber bowed her head for a moment, the long curtain of her hair hiding her face from his glittering gaze. She squeezed her eyes tightly shut to hold back the tears. She disgusted him, he had said, and yet she was only what he had made her, and in that instant the new Amber was born.

Swiping back the mass of hair from her face, she rose to her feet. Ignoring Lucas's looming presence, she picked up her briefs and leggings and, turning her back on him, took her time about putting them on. Then, straightening her shoulders, she turned to face him.

She lifted hard golden eyes to his. 'What are you waiting for?' she demanded bluntly. She was furiously angry at the undisguised contempt in his expression. But she refused to show it. 'I thought a man of your high moral values would be long gone,' she mocked him. She had learnt her lesson well. Never again in this life, she vowed, would she show any man how she really felt.

'The floor show is over,' she said facetiously. 'If you're hoping for a repeat performance, forget it—go back to Christina and I wish you both joy. Though I have a suspicion you will not find her quite the pure, malleable little bed partner and wife you imagine. After all, she already knows you have a mistress—' she wanted to hurt him, dent his arrogant pride '—and she doesn't care, which must tell you something.'

She had gone too far. He stepped towards her, his hand lifted as if to hit her. Involuntarily she flinched and stepped back.

'No.' His hand fell to his side, his fingers curling into a fist, his knuckles white with strain. 'You are a lying little bitch.' Amber knew he would never believe her or forgive her for her comments. 'And you will never speak to my fiancée or mention her name again.'

Amber stared at him, her anger dying fast as his glance roamed contemptuously over her. There was sheer hatred in his eyes, and a clear message he would not touch her again if his life depended on it. But then she already knew that, she thought sadly. The last half-hour had been nothing more than animal attraction fuelled by rage on his part. He didn't want her love, never had... The realisation was the end of everything for Amber. 'Just go,' she said wearily, brushing past him towards the door. Good manners decreed she see him out, she thought, and had to choke back hysterical laughter.

She opened the door and held it. Lucas reached out to grasp her arm, but she pulled away. 'Goodbye, Lucas.' The finality in her tone was unmistakable.

He went rigid. 'Not so fast, you still have not given me the promise I asked for. I...I want your word you will not marry Spiro.'

She was sick at heart and halfway to being physically sick. 'Okay.'

'I mean it, Amber,' Lucas said with deadly emphasis. 'If you marry him your life will not be worth living, and you will find no solace in your work, that I promise.' The taut line of his mouth gave way to a thin cruel smile as he paused. 'I will personally make sure no one in the financial world will ever employ you again.' He had to convince her for his own sanity to break all ties with Spiro. If the last hour had taught him anything it was that there was no way on God's earth Lucas trusted himself to be in the company of Amber ever again. Not even a simple social occasion, or he was in danger of succumbing to the same sickening addiction to sex his mother had suffered from. The realisation of his own weakness shocked and horrified him, and he reacted with the same icy determination that made him a ruthlessly successful businessman. 'I will totally destroy the career you love, and, believe me, I can and will do it.'

It was no idle threat, and the really scary part was that Amber had no doubt he could destroy her career with a few chosen words to her most influential clients. 'Your threat is unnecessary. I have no intention of marrying Spiro.'

Amber's golden gaze roamed over Lucas as though she were seeing him for the first time. He stood in the entrance door, tall and broad and as still as a statue carved in stone. She registered the soft wool sweater moulding the muscles of his broad chest, the hip-hugging jeans. Raising her gaze, she noted the thick black hair, the broad forehead, the perfectly chiselled features—he was incredibly handsome, but his face was hard, cold, the inner man hidden. One thumb casually hooked his leather jacket over a shoulder, but there was nothing casual about the man. Spiro had called him a shark and Amber finally realised it was true.

It was a revelation to Amber's bruised heart. Lucas thought he loved Christina, but it was not what Amber considered love to be. It was no great consuming passion on Lucas's part, he was incapable of the emotion. He had simply planned to fall in love with Christina with the same ruthless efficiency he planned a takeover bid. Christina simply met his criteria for a wife. Amber's golden eyes met his, black and not a glimmer of human warmth in their depths, just a ruthless determination to succeed be it business or private, family or friend. He was incapable of differentiating between them. How had she ever thought she loved this cold, frighteningly austere man?

'If you knew your nephew a little better, or at all,' Amber said softly, one perfectly arched brow lifting eloquently, 'you would have realised he was only winding you up when he said it. Now please go.'

With the door closed behind him, Amber silently added, If Lucas allowed anyone to know him, he might possibly develop into a halfway decent human being. But she had a suspicion he never had, and he was too old to change now.

Three weeks later in the same Monday morning paper Amber viewed the wedding photo of Lucas and Christina with a cynical smile. She read the gossip that went with it, the gist of it being that there were great celebrations at the high society wedding in Athens and the joining together of two great Greek families, not to mention the amalgamation of two international corporations to make one of the top leisure companies in the world.

Amber settled into her small house, bought a neat Ford car to drive into work, and as the days and weeks went past tried to put her disastrous love affair out of her mind. During the day she could block Lucas out of her thoughts with work. But at night she was haunted by memories of the sheer magic of his lovemaking—only it hadn't been love, she had to keep reminding herself, and then the tears would fall. The only thing that kept Amber from a nervous breakdown over the next year was her growing relationship with her father. The news she had wanted to tell Lucas so eagerly, after lunching with Sir David Janson.

Two weeks after Lucas Karadines had left her, Amber had met Sir David again for lunch at a restaurant in Covent Garden. Much to Amber's surprise his wife Mildred had accompanied him. It could have been embarrassing, but Mildred quickly explained she did not blame her husband or Amber's mother. At the time Mildred had left her husband and two children and had lived with another man for over a year. Sir David had found solace with his secretary and Amber was the result.

Sir David quite happily acknowledged Amber as his daughter, saying a certain notorious Member of Parliament had recognised an illegitimate daughter without any ill effect, so why shouldn't he? It was a one-day wonder in the papers, and his family—a married daughter and a much older son—were equally welcoming.

But Amber refused to take a job with her father's company. Her feminine intuition told her she shouldn't. Sir David's son, Mark Janson, accepted her in the family, but as heir apparent to the business he was nowhere near so happy about having her in his father's firm. Especially as Sir David told all and sundry Amber had obviously inherited her skill in the money markets from him.

CHAPTER FIVE

FIVE years later...

As Monday mornings went, this had to be one of the worst, Amber thought sadly. She'd just returned from two weeks' holiday in Tuscany at her father's villa feeling relaxed, and revitalised. June in Italy was beautiful; unfortunately June in London was rain, the stock market had dropped three per cent, and now this...

Her long fingers tapped restlessly on the document lying on the desk. She'd read the letter countless times, but she still could not quite believe it. The letter was from a firm of lawyers in New York, the lawyers dealing with the estate of the late Spiro Karadines. It was dated eleven days ago. Spiro had died the day before, apparently, and it was informing her of the time and place of his funeral in Greece, and a legal document in the usual lawyer speak that 'Amber Jackson may learn something to her advantage'. Amber didn't think so... Spiro was trouble...

A sad, reminiscent smile curved her wide mouth. It was four years since she'd last seen him, and they had not parted on the best of terms.

She had gone to New York for the grand opening of his art gallery. Spiro had been so excited as he had shown Amber around the exhibition. It had been incredible, or perhaps unbelievable was a better word, Amber had thought privately. Spiro had told her the artists whose work was on display were all up and coming in the modern art world. To Amber's untrained eyes it looked more as if they had been and gone... Gone crazy...

'Are you sure about this stuff?' she had asked Spiro, recoiling from a massive red and green painting that appeared to be bits of body parts.

'Yes, don't worry, in half an hour people will be fighting over these paintings. Trust me!'

Her smooth brow pleated in a frown as she fiddled with the letter on her desk. She'd trusted Spiro when he had assured her that if she gave him the money from the sale of the loft apartment to start his art gallery, he would never tell Lucas, and return it with interest when he came into his inheritance a year later. He had persuaded her that charity could wait, and, being honest, Amber admitted she had thought it was poetic justice, letting Spiro have the money as it was Karadines money after all. He had also told her Lucas would not be at the opening. Spiro had lied on both counts...

Although it had been over a year since she'd last seen Lucas, the gut-wrenching pain she had felt when she'd turned around from viewing the 'Body Parts' painting to find him, and Christina his wife, his *pregnant* wife, standing behind her had been almost unbearable.

She'd glanced at Spiro, and seen the devilment in his eyes, and known he had done it deliberately. Shifting her gaze to the couple, she'd made the obligatory greeting portraying a sophistication she had not felt. She'd even managed to congratulate the pair on their forthcoming happy event. But she'd been shaken so badly she'd had to clasp her hands behind her back to hide their trembling.

But Lucas had had no such problem. His eyes had slid over her with cool insolence, stripping away the stylish green silk sheath dress she'd worn to the flesh beneath, but Amber had forced herself to withstand his scrutiny, and done some scrutinising of her own. Thick dark hair had curled down over the collar of his impeccably tailored light linen suit, he'd been leaner than he had been the last time she had seen him, his features slightly more fine drawn, but as devastatingly attractive as ever, until he'd spoken.

'It seems congratulations are in order for you too, Amber. Spiro tells me you are his partner and put up most of the money for this little venture,' Lucas said smoothly. 'A remarkable achievement for a young woman. Your passion...' his hesitation was deliberate '...for finance must be truly exceptional,' he opined with mocking cynicism.

Amber felt the colour burn up under her skin. Lucas wasn't referring only to her passion for business. He obviously knew where the money had come from and for a moment she felt like strangling Spiro. But instead she forced herself to look at Lucas. 'Luckily I seem to have a gift for it.' Amber stared at him, deliberately holding his eyes. 'But I'll never be in your league. Men have a certain ruthlessness...' and it was her turn to pause '...in business, women find hard to emulate.'

'Not all women,' Lucas said flatly, and Amber surprised what looked very much like a flicker of regret in his dark eyes before he turned his attention to his wife, and began a conversation in Greek, ignoring Amber completely.

Instead of being insulted Amber was glad to escape the attention of Lucas; breathing an inward sigh of relief, she turned away. It hurt her more than she wanted to admit to see the two of them so close, and she was going to have a very serious talk to her so-called partner. Spiro was talking animatedly to a guest in the now crowded gallery. He could wait!

Spying Tim, she'd begun to walk towards him when suddenly someone grabbed her bare arm. The tingling sensation of the long fingers on her bare flesh was electric. Lucas...

'What?' Amber snapped.

'Will you follow Christina to the rest room, make sure she is all right?' he asked, his expression one of deep concern, the worry in his dark eyes there for all to see as they tracked his wife heading for the powder room.

Amber did see. His request reinforced what she had tried to deny. Amazing for such a predatory male, Lucas, a man who was ruthless in the business world, a man whom she'd thought incapable of love, was actually madly in love with his wife.

'She is pregnant, not sick.' Amber shrugged off his hand and stalked away without looking back. Listening to Christina rhapsodising about Lucas and the soon-to-be family was the last thing she needed. Lucas was a fantastic lover, and, once Christina had discovered the wonder to be found in her husband's arms, she had to have fallen in love with him, even if she had not been at the beginning.

After a furious row with Spiro, Amber left New York the next day, and she had not seen or spoken to Spiro since. As for the money she had given him, she had written that off long ago.

With the benefit of hindsight Amber had come to realise that Lucas had been right about Spiro. She should never have given him the money, because within a week of the gallery opening Tim and Spiro had split up. Spiro had been having an affair with the artist of 'Body Parts'.

Tim had returned to England, and back to his home in Northumbria. Six months later he had received a brief note, not from Spiro, but from a New York clinic telling him to get himself tested. Spiro had been HIV positive, as had been the artist lover who had somehow forgotten to mention the fact!

Restlessly Amber swivelled around in her chair, and stared out of the plate-glass window of her office, not really seeing what was beyond. She felt guilty and half blamed herself for Spiro's illness. If she hadn't given him the money, he would not have gone to New York, and it might never have happened.

Tim was a successful wildlife artist living and working from his home in the north and perfectly healthy. He had told her over and over again, it was not her fault Spiro had done what he had. Tim firmly believed Amber and himself had both fallen victims to the charm of the Karadines men; it was that simple, and they had both had a lucky escape.

Swivelling back to face her desk, Amber picked up the telephone and dialled Tim's number in Thropton. He had a right to know Spiro was dead.

The conversation was not as difficult as she had expected. Tim was quite philosophical about it: the past was past—so they had lost a good friend, but in reality they had lost him years ago.

'You're right, Tim...' Suddenly her office door swung open and someone walked in unannounced. Amber lifted her head. Recognition was instant, her golden eyes widening in shock. 'I'll see you soon, love,' she finished her conversation, and replaced the receiver.

She was thankful she was sitting down because she doubted her legs would support her. Lucas Karadines... She didn't dare meet his cold black eyes, and, carefully taking deep breaths, she sought to calm her suddenly erratic pulse. She should have expected this as soon as she had read the line 'something to her advantage' she realised too late.

He was standing in the middle of her office as though he owned the place. Amber's first thought was that Lucas at forty-one looked little different than he had done when they had first met. His body beneath the conservatively tailored charcoal-grey suit was still lithe and firm, his face was still handsome, but the harsh symmetry of bones and flesh mirrored a cold bitterness that she had never noticed before. He looked lean and as predatory as ever, but he looked older, harder than she would have expected for a happily married man, was her second thought. The lines bracketing his mouth were deeper, the hair at his temples liberally streaked with silver. But nothing could detract from the aura of dynamic, vibrant male he wore like a powerful cloak, masking his ruthlessly chauvinistic nature. He would be a handsome devil to his dying day, Amber acknowledged wryly.

Amber felt colour creeping under her skin as he made no immediate attempt to either move or speak. His hands were slanted casually into his trouser pockets, accentuating the musculature of his long legs. His eyes were hooded so she could not tell what he was thinking as they slid slowly over her head and shoulders to where the collar of her blue silk blouse revealed a glimpse of cleavage. She fought the impulse to slip her suit jacket off the back of the chair and put it on. This was her office, and Lucas was the intruder, and as he made no attempt to break the tense silence between them she finally found her voice.

'What do you want?' she asked abruptly.

Lucas Karadines for the first time in his life was struck dumb. The instant tightening in his groin shocked him into silence. His body had not reacted this way in years. His memory of Amber had not done her justice. She'd matured into the most exquisitely beautiful woman he had ever seen. His dark eyes drank in the sight of her. The hair scraped back from her face only accentuated the perfection of her features, the elegant line of her throat, the shadowed cleft between her luscious breasts her conservative blouse could not quite hide.

'Not a great welcome for an old friend,' Lucas finally murmured, his dark eyes gleaming with mockery, before scanning the elegant office. 'So this is your domain.'

A corner suite with windows on two sides, it was light and airy, and in keeping with her present position in the firm as the youngest partner, and Amber was justifiably proud of her achievements. 'Obviously,' she said dryly.

'You have done well for yourself, but then I always said you would.' Lucas's glance skimmed lightly over her desk as he moved towards it, noting her hand still on the phone. 'Sorry if I interrupted your conversation with your lover, but you and I have some pressing business to discuss.'

Her hand gripping the telephone was white-knuckled, and, realising she was betraying her shock, she smoothly slipped her hands to her lap and managed to smile coolly back at him. She was fiercely glad that the sophisticate she had pretended to be when they had first met was now a reality. She refused to be intimidated by Lucas—or any man, for that matter.

'I can't imagine we have anything to discuss, Mr Karadines. As far as I am aware you are a client of Janson's and I am not in the habit of poaching my father's clients.' It gave her great satisfaction to say it. Whether Lucas was aware Sir David was her father, she did not know. But she was making it abundantly clear he was not about to treat her like some inferior being to be discarded like yesterday's newspaper as he had before.

'Yes, I heard. I'm surprised you didn't choose to join Sir David's firm,' he opined smoothly. 'I seem to remember Clive Thompson was rather keen on the idea.'

'He still is,' Amber shot back, angry that Lucas had the nerve to remind her of that horrible party. 'But I like it at Brentford's and I don't believe in nepotism,' she said with a shrug. 'Nor mixing business with pleasure.' Let him make of that what he liked. She'd been dating Clive for the past year and part of the reason she had spent the last couple of weeks on holiday was to decide if she should accept Clive's proposal of marriage.

'Very wise of you. I dispensed with their services myself some months ago.'

That did surprise her. Neither Clive nor Mark, her half-brother, who had been the head of the firm since their father had retired two years ago, had mentioned the fact.

'I didn't know,' she said blandly, implying that she didn't really care.

'Now, if there is nothing further, I am rather busy.' Tilting back her head, she stared up at him, deliberately holding his eyes. 'And it is usual to make an appointment.' The sarcasm in her tone was very evident. 'I am a busy lady.'

Lucas was not the slightest bit fazed. 'I'm sure you are, Amber—a little too busy, it would seem.'

Amber raised her eyebrows. 'Too busy, says a man who was the most driven, competitive workaholic!' she mocked lightly. 'Marriage has changed you. How is the family? Well, I hope.' She was proud of her ability to ask the conventional question, and was surprised to realise it actually did not hurt at all.

Lucas stilled, his handsome face as expressionless as stone. 'I have no family. Spiro was the last—that is why I am here.'

Amber's face went white. Oh, God! In her shock at seeing Lucas again, she had forgotten all about Spiro's death. How could she have been so callous? 'I'm sorry, Lucas, truly sorry,' she hastened into an explanation. 'I only found out this morning. I've been on holiday, and the news hasn't really sunk in yet. I'm sorry I missed the funeral. Please sit down.' She indicated a chair at the opposite side of the desk with the wave of her hand. 'I'll order some coffee.' She was babbling, she knew, and, pressing for her secretary, she quickly asked Sandy to bring in two coffees.

He lowered his long length into the chair she had indicated. 'Cut out the phoney sympathy, Amber,' he commanded bluntly. 'We both know Spiro hated my guts, and the fact he left everything he possessed to you simply underlined the fact.'

'He what?' she exclaimed, her golden eyes widening in astonishment on Lucas's hard face, and what she saw in his night-black eyes sent a shiver of something very like fear quivering down her spine. 'No, I don't believe you,' she amended quickly. 'Spiro wouldn't.' Then she remembered the 'something to her advantage'.

'Yes, Spiro would, and did, and your innocent act does not impress me,' he said harshly. 'You knew damn fine you stood to inherit Spiro's share of the business.'

'Now wait just a minute—' Amber began, but at that moment Sandy walked in with the coffee.

Amber sat bristling with frustration as she watched her secretary, the girl's eyes awestruck as she asked Lucas breathlessly how he took his coffee.

'Black, please.' He favoured her with a broad smile and just sat looking dark and strikingly attractive until the flustered girl handed him a cup of coffee. 'Thank you.'

Amber thought Sandy was going to swoon. No wonder she had let Lucas in without an appointment. Even her secretary, who had only been married a few months, was not immune to Lucas's lethal male charm.

When Amber had first seen Lucas walk into her office she had been in shock, but now the shock had worn off, and another much more dangerous emotion was threatening her hard-won equilibrium. Lucas was a handsome devil and he still had the power to stir her feminine hormones.

Amber hastily picked up her cup of coffee and took a long drink of the reviving brew. The days were long gone when she was a slave to the sexual excitement Lucas could arouse with a mere look or touch. He had killed them dead when he had accused her of being an oversexed female, excellent lover material, but never a wife, and then had gone off and married Christina.

For months after his desertion her self-esteem had hit rock-bottom. She'd questioned her own worth; perhaps Lucas had been right about her. She was sex mad, the hedonist he had called her. She certainly had been when she'd been with him. In consequence she had, without really being aware of doing it, adjusted her style of dress to elegant but conservative—no short skirts, or revealing necklines. She wore little make-up and kept her long hair ruthlessly scraped back in a tight chignon, and she had no idea she looked even more desirable.

The door closing as Sandy left brought Amber back to the present with a start, and, straightening her shoulders, she was once again in command. She looked at Lucas with narrowed hostile eyes. 'I don't need you to tell me what I do or don't know,' she said curtly, and, picking up the letter from the desk, she held it out to him.

'Read that. I saw it for the first time this morning, and as yet I have not had time to respond, basically because I have an unscheduled guest. You.' His fingers brushed hers as he took the document from her outstretched hand, igniting a tingling sensation on her soft skin. Her golden eyes narrowed warily to his face, sure he had done it deliberately, but he was unfolding the document.

She waited as he read the letter, and then with slow deliberation folded the document back up again. 'This proves nothing,' Lucas said bluntly, dropping the letter back on her desk.

'I don't have to prove anything to you, Mr Karadines.' She shrugged dismissively. 'Now finish your coffee and leave. I have work to do.' Yes, Amber congratulated herself, she was back on track; the cool businesswoman. 'And when I get around to contacting the lawyers, and discover the true state of affairs, then if I need to get in touch with you, I will.' When hell freezes over, she thought silently. Standing up, she drained her coffee-cup and replaced it on the desk, before walking around heading for the door, her intention to show Lucas out as swiftly as possible.

'Well, well. The hard-bitten businesswoman act,' Lucas drawled sardonically, rising to his feet, and when she moved to pass him he reached out for her.

Amber felt every hair on her skin leaping to attention as his long fingers encircled her forearm. 'It is no act. Believe me!' she retaliated sharply. If he thought he was going to walk all over her again, he was in for a rude awakening.

'You don't fool me, Amber.' His voice dropped throatily, his fingers tightening ever so slightly on her arm. His eyes wandered over her in blatant masculine appraisal, taking in the prim neckline of her blue blouse, the tailored navy blue trousers that skimmed her slender hips and concealed her long legs to the classic low-heeled navy shoes, and then ever so slowly back to her face until she thought she would scream with the effort to remain cool and in control. 'You may dress like a conservative businesswoman, but it doesn't change what you are. I always knew you had a passion for sex, but it was only after we parted that I realised you had an equal passion for money,' he drawled cynically.

She wrenched her arm free from his hold, her whole

body rigid with anger. Just who the hell did he think he was? So now she was a gold-digger, as well as a sex maniac in his eyes... With the greatest effort of will, Amber managed to control her fury and say calmly, 'What exactly do you want, Lucas, barging into my office un-announced? I have neither the time nor the inclination for playing games. You obviously know something about Spiro's will, which concerns me. So just spit it out and then go.'

His eyes darkened, and for a moment Amber saw a flash of violent anger in their glittering depths, and she knew she had been right to feel threatened. Then he was smiling mockingly down at her. 'You used to like playing games,' he reminded her, his eyes cruel. 'Sexual games.' His finger lifted and stroked down the curve of her cheek.

'Cut that out,' she snapped, taking a deep, shuddering breath. 'You're a married man, remember.' Her golden eyes clashed with his, and as she watched it was like a shutter falling down over his face.

Lucas's hand fell from her face, his black eyes cold and blank. 'No, I am not. I told you before, I have no family.'

Confusion flickered in Amber's eyes. Had he? Then she remembered, but she had thought he'd meant Spiro. 'But what about Christina and your child?'

'The child was stillborn. My father died three years ago, and Christina was gone the next,' he informed her in clipped tones.

Her soft heart flooded with compassion, and unthink-ingly she laid a hand on his arm in a tender gesture... Such tragedy must be heartbreaking even for a man as hard as Lucas. 'I am so sorry, Lucas, I had no idea.'

'These things happen...' he brushed her hand away '...and, as you never cared much for any of them, I can do without your hypocritical sympathy. I would ask you not to mention the subject again. Except for *Spiro*, of course,' he demanded with chilling emphasis.

Why was she wasting her sympathy on this man? Lucas meant nothing to her. He was simply another irritant in an already bad day, she told herself. So why did her cheek still burn where he had touched her, her pulse still race? It wasn't fair that one man could have such a terrible effect on her senses. She glanced up at him, and briefly his towering presence was a threat to her hard-won sophistication, then she casually took a step back.

'You want to talk about Spiro, fire away,' she said flatly, retreating behind her usual hard shell of astute business-woman, and deliberately she lifted her wrist and scanned the elegant gold watch she wore. 'But make it quick, I have a lunch appointment.'

'You have changed, Amber.' His lips quirked in the semblance of a smile that did not quite reach his eyes. 'I can remember a time when you begged for my company, you couldn't get enough of me and pleaded with me to stay with you,' he said silkily.

The unexpected personal attack made her go white, a terrible coldness invading her very being that he could be so utterly callous as to mention the last time they had been alone together. 'I can't,' she denied flatly. He might even now make her heart race, but no way was she foolish enough to get personal with Lucas Karadines ever again.

'Liar.' He smiled sardonically. 'But I'll let it go for now, as you say you are busy, and we have a much more pressing item to discuss, *partner*.'

'Partner.' She bristled. What on earth was the man talking about? She'd rather partner a rattlesnake.

'All right, pretend you're innocent, I don't really care. But, put simply, the will Spiro made when you invested in his art gallery made you his heir if anything happened to him.'

'Oh, no!' Amber exclaimed, a horrible suspicion making her face pale. It couldn't be. But one look at Lucas's dark countenance confirmed her worst fear. When she had given Spiro the money he had insisted on making a will naming her his heir as collateral for the loan, until he could pay her back.

'Oh, ye-es,' Lucas drawled derisively. 'Spiro never changed his will. You are now, or very soon will be, the proud owner of a substantial part of Karadines.'

He was watching her with eyes that glittered with undisguised contempt and something else she could not put a name to.

Amber simply stared at him like a paralysed porpoise, her mouth hanging open in shocked horror. How typical of Spiro. He would get a bee in his bonnet about something, do it and then forget all about it. His business sense had always been negligible, but Amber hadn't seen it until it was too late.

Lucas laughed, but there was no humour in it. 'Struck dumb; how very typical of you. The silent treatment might have worked for you in the past with Spiro,' Lucas drawled, a smile creasing his firm mouth, 'but not this time. I am a totally different male animal to my late nephew.'

He'd got that right! Amber had a hysterical desire to laugh—a more ruggedly aggressive macho male than Lucas would be impossible to find. Her lips quirked, while she damned Spiro for landing her in this mess.

'You find something amusing in this situation?' he challenged icily.

The ring of the telephone saved her from answering. 'Yes, Sandy, what is it?' she asked briskly. 'Clive.' She glanced sideways at Lucas and caught a thunderous frown on his dark face.

'Tell him two minutes, my client is just leaving,' she informed Sandy before turning towards Lucas. 'My lunch date has arrived, I'm afraid I must ask you to leave.'

'Clive Thompson, I might have guessed—he was lusting after you the first time he met you,' Lucas opined bluntly. His dark eyes swept over her cynically. Her wide, oddly coloured gold eyes, and the full sensual lips that begged to be kissed. Her startling beauty combined with a slender yet curvaceous body was enough to make a grown man ache. Lucas was aching and he bitterly resented it. 'Obviously he has succeeded, but by your ringless fingers I see you have had no success getting him to the altar yet,' he taunted.

The arrogant bastard, Amber thought angrily. He was still of the opinion she was good enough to bed, but not to wed. Well, he was in for a big surprise.

'Ah, Lucas, that is where you are wrong.' Amber smiled a deliberately slow, sexy curve of her full lips. 'Clive appreciates my talents.' Let the swine make of that whatever his lecherous mind concluded. 'He has asked me to marry him, but I have yet to give him my answer—perhaps over lunch,' she said. 'So, if you will excuse me.'

He moved so fast Amber didn't have time to avoid him. One minute there were six feet of space between them, and the next she was hauled against the hard-muscled wall of his chest. Before she could struggle, one large hand slipped down over her buttocks, pressing hard against his thighs, and she felt the heat of him searing into her even through her clothes. 'No, I won't excuse you,' he rasped.

Amber's throat closed in panic. The years since they had last met might never have been. It was as if Lucas had rolled back time, his sexuality so potent that it fired her blood, making her once again the young girl who had been a slave to her senses. Then his dark head descended and he kissed her.

'Lucas, no,' she managed to croak as his mouth plundered hers, as he ground the tender flesh of her lips back against her teeth in a brutal travesty of a loving kiss. But even as she hated him, her body flooded with a feverish excitement and she fought the compulsion to surrender with every ounce of will-power she possessed, but it was not enough. The sexual chemistry between them had always been explosive. The years had not dulled the effect, and with a hoarse moan she responded. Lucas's hold relaxed as he sensed her surrender, and, realising how completely she had betrayed herself, she swiftly twisted out of his arms.

'Get out,' she ordered in a voice that shook, her arms folded protectively across her breasts as she put as much space between them as her office allowed.

'*Christo!* It was only a kiss—since when have you ever objected to a kiss?' he derided savagely. 'I was wrong, you haven't changed. You can't help responding. It is to be hoped Clive knows what he is taking on.'

The cruelty of his attack drove every last vestige of colour from her face.

His narrowed eyes studied her pale face for a long moment before a self-satisfied smile tilted the corners of his mouth. 'Well, well, you haven't told Clive about you and I.' He was far too astute; he had seen the answer in her lowered gaze.

Lifting her head, she looked straight at him. 'There is no you and I,' she declared angrily. 'There never was, as you were at great pains to point out when you married Christina.' Her eyes sparkled with cold defiance.

His temper rose as swiftly as her own. 'Leave Christina

out of this,' he commanded. 'And if you want Clive to stay in ignorance...' he paused, his narrowed gaze cold on her lovely face '...you will have dinner with me tonight. I will pick you up here at six and we will continue our talk. We have a lot to discuss.'

Panicked by his kiss, her lips tingling with the taste of him, Amber had forgotten Lucas's real reason for seeking her out. There was still the will to discuss...

'All right,' she said curtly. 'I'll check with New York this afternoon. The sooner this matter is settled, the better.' The thought of Lucas back in her life filled her with horror and fear.

'Amber, darling.' Clive strolled into the office, saw Lucas and stopped. 'Lucas Karadines.' And he held out his hand for Lucas to shake. 'Thinking of changing bankers yet again?' Clive asked conversationally.

'No, nothing like that. A private matter concerning my late nephew Spiro. Now, if you will excuse me...' Lucas glanced at Amber, his dark eyes holding a definite threat '...until later.' And he left.

Clive quickly crossed to Amber's side, and put a comforting arm around her shoulder. 'I forgot to tell you when I spoke to you yesterday. I heard about Spiro a week ago. I know he used to be a good friend of yours; it must have been a shock.'

A tragedy. A calamity that Amber had a sinking feeling was only going to get worse.

Lunch was a disaster. Amber toyed with the food on her plate, her mind in turmoil. One kiss from Lucas Karadines, and her carefully considered decision taken after two weeks in Italy to accept Clive's proposal of marriage was shot to hell...

Clive was very understanding when she told him she needed more time. But she saw the hurt in his blue eyes when they said goodbye outside her office building, and she hated herself for it. He was a true friend.

CHAPTER SIX

RETURNING from lunch, Amber stopped at her secretary's desk. 'Sandy...' she looked hard at the pretty brunette '...what possessed you to let Mr Karadines walk straight into my office? You know the rules. No one gets in unless they have an appointment, especially not Mr Karadines, you must inform me first. Do I make myself clear?'

'Sorry.' Sandy apologised and then grinned. 'But he said he was an old friend and he wanted to surprise you, and I couldn't resist. I thought you would be pleased. I know *I* would. Smart, charming and sexy as hell; what more could a girl want?'

'He is also a domineering, chauvinistic pig, with the mind-set of a medieval monarch,' Amber declared with a wry grin. Sandy was an excellent secretary but a hopeless romantic. 'Now get back to work,' Amber commanded and walked into her office, closing the door behind her. She couldn't blame Sandy. Lucas had a lethal charm that few women, if any, could resist...

A fax to New York was her first priority and then Amber spent all afternoon trying to work, but without accomplishing much. It was five in the afternoon when she finally received a reply to her fax. She read it, and groaned; her worst fear was confirmed. Lucas, damn him, was right! She was Spiro's sole heir, and clarification of what that entailed would follow by mail.

Amber did not need to know. She'd made up her mind that whatever Spiro had left her she would give to Lucas. She wanted nothing to do with Karadines ever again...

She'd been badly burnt once and only a fool put their hand in the flame a second time. Ruthlessly she squashed the wayward thought that Lucas was a single man once more. He probably wasn't, she thought dryly. Lucas had a powerful sex drive, he was not the sort to do without a woman for very long, and there were millions of women out there only too ready to fall into bed with the man.

She was walking out of her personal washroom when the telephone rang. Crossing to her desk, she pressed the button on the intercom to hear Sandy at her most formal announcing the arrival of Mr Karadines.

'Send him in,' Amber responded briskly.

A moment later with an exaggerated flourish Sandy flung the door wide open. 'Lucas Karadines.' Strolling past Sandy, Lucas gave the girl a smile and a thank-you.

Even though Amber was ready for him, her heart still missed a beat, and anger with herself made her tone sharp. 'Thanks, Sandy, you can leave now. I will see Mr Karadines out myself.'

'As I have no intention of leaving without you, your last statement was rather superfluous, wouldn't you say?' Lucas queried sardonically.

Amber forced herself to meet the mockery she knew would be in his eyes. 'Not at all. I think when you hear what I have to say, this meeting will be over in a few minutes.' She was slightly reassured when she realised he was still wearing the same charcoal suit as before. Like her, he had not bothered to change; with a bit of luck, she could avoid having dinner with him.

'Really?' he drawled silkily. 'You intrigue me.'

'Yes, well. I have checked with New York, you were right about Spiro's will. I don't have the details yet, but it does not matter, because I have decided to sign everything over to you.'

'Such generosity, Amber.' He was laughing at her, she could see it in the sparkle in his black eyes. 'But then you were always very generous, at least in one department,' Lucas drawled softly, a flick of his lashes sending his gaze skimming over her with deliberate sensual provocation.

She shivered, with what must be cold, she told herself as she stared at him in silence for a second, then lowered her gaze to the desk and picked up her briefcase. She was over Lucas. She had been for years. He had humiliated her, and caused her more pain than any woman should have to bear. So why? Why did the sight of him, the sound of him, still have the power to disturb her? With no answer, she continued as though he had never spoken.

'That being the case, I don't think there is anything for us to discuss at this time. When I am in possession of the full facts of Spiro's legacy, I'll have my lawyer contact yours as soon as possible.' Clutching her briefcase, she stepped forward, about to stalk past him, but his hand reached out and his fingers bit into her shoulder. Instinctively she froze.

'It is not that simple, Amber, and you promised to join me for dinner,' he reminded her pointedly. 'I'm holding you to that.'

She wanted to deny him, but his closeness, his hand on her shoulder were a brittle reminder of her own susceptibility to the man. She was not indifferent to Lucas, no matter how much she tried to deny it. Whenever he came near her she was rigid with tension. Her heart pounded and her mouth went dry, a throwback to the time they'd spent together, and something she'd thought she'd got over long ago.

'If you insist,' Amber managed to say coolly, and, shrugging her shoulder, she slipped from under his restraining hand. 'But it is totally unnecessary. I've told you, you can have the lot.'

'If only it were that easy. You're a businesswoman, Amber, you should know better,' Lucas opined sarcastically. 'But now is not the time to discuss it. Unlike you, I missed lunch and I'm starving. Let's go.'

She didn't really want to go anywhere with Lucas, but one glance at his granite-like profile and she knew it would be futile to argue. Much better to go along with him now, than put off the discussion to another day. 'Okay,' she agreed, and preceded him out of the office. Entering the lift, she tried to ignore Lucas's brooding presence lounging against one wall, apparently content to remain silent now he had got his own way.

Her mother had always told her it was better to take bad medicine in one go, and Lucas was certainly that where she was concerned. How bad could it be? A couple of hours in his company and then she never need see him again. Amber consoled herself with the thought as the lift hummed silently to the ground floor, and she stepped out into the foyer, her chin up, her expression one of cool control.

'There is quite a nice little Italian restaurant just around the corner from here,' she offered with a brief glance at Lucas, tall and indomitable at her side.

'No, I have already made arrangements.'

Amber shot him a sharp glance. She didn't like the sound of that, but as they were exiting the building the early rain had given way to brilliant sun and dazzled her eyes for a moment. When she did focus, Lucas was opening the door of a black BMW parked illegally at the kerb.

She stopped. 'I have my own car, tell me where we are going and I'll follow you.'

'Not necessary. Get in, I can see a traffic warden coming.' His large hand grasped hers, urging her forward. 'Don't worry, I'll bring you back.'

Amber didn't want to get in his car, but a brief glance along the road told her he was telling the truth, at least about the traffic warden, so she did as she was told. It was only as he deftly manoeuvred the car through the rush-hour traffic that she realised to a man of his wealth a traffic ticket was nothing. When he stopped the car outside the impressive entrance to the Karadines Hotel, Amber's face paled. Lucas had to be the most insensitive man alive, or else he had brought her here deliberately and was just plain cruel.

'Why here?' Amber queried as Lucas helped her out of the car. She didn't want to put her hand in his, but she did, refusing to let him see how much he still affected her. 'Not very discreet of you.'

'It is too late for discretion, you own part of the place.' Lucas's hard, intent gaze held hers. 'So follow my lead and behave.'

She stared at him, their eyes warring for a second, and she was the first to look away. 'All right.'

The foyer was relatively empty, but even so the hotel manager appeared and greeted Lucas effusively. Amber, to her consternation, was urged forward and Lucas insisted on introducing her to the man as a partner in the business.

'What did you do that for?' she snapped as soon as the man took his leave of them. 'I have not the least intention of—'

'Keep it till we get to the suite.'

'Wait a minute. I am not going to any suite with you.' She stopped dead and looked up into his cold dark eyes. 'The restaurant will do perfectly well.'

'And run the risk of some employee tuning into our

business discussion?' he drawled sardonically. 'I think not, Amber.'

'Then you should not have brought me here in the first place,' she snapped.

Lucas's dark head bent towards her. 'I thought you would appreciate somewhere you knew,' he suggested softly, his breath feathering across her cheek as his hand settled in the middle of her back and he urged her across to the bank of lifts and into a conveniently empty one.

'You thought wrong,' she declared angrily, twisting away from his hand, her body taut with tension. She stared at his broad back as he pressed the required button and the doors closed, entombing them in the small space.

Slowly Lucas turned and lounged back against the carpeted wall, his dark eyes narrowing speculatively on her furious face. 'It can't be the place, because you are familiar with the hotel. So why the anger, Amber? I could almost believe you are afraid of me.'

He hadn't moved, but all at once the atmosphere had become charged with sexual tension. Amber's mouth was dry, the blood moving rapidly through her veins. 'I'm not afraid of any man.' She raised her eyebrows, her air of sophistication firmly back in place. 'And I am not familiar with the hotel,' she said sweetly. 'I have only been here twice, and *both* times were a disaster. The first you dragged me into bed, and the second you drove me out.' She managed to say it all with a light, even tone of voice, and she watched with interest as a red tide of colour ran up under his skin. 'Or had you forgotten in the old days you had a preference for discreet little restaurants, as I suggested earlier?'

The lift came to a halt, and Amber had the distinct impression Lucas was relieved he did not have to respond. Stroke one up for her, she thought irreverently as she followed him down a short corridor, and brushed past the door he held open for her without a glance.

The elegant sitting room was exactly the same with its luxury fitted carpet and period furniture. The large patio doors leading out onto the terrace were wide open and she had a glimpse of a table set for two. Some of her hard-won sophistication evaporated as she recalled the only other time she had been in this suite. The first time they had made love.

She stared at the floor with unseeing eyes. She had been a virgin, and totally ignorant of the power of love. She had been shy at first but so desperately eager. She felt the colour rise in her cheeks at the memory. A few passionate kisses and he had carried her into the bedroom and she had let him strip her naked—helped him, in fact. Then he had told her to undress him, and she had fumblingly complied. With breathtaking expertise he had taken her to the heights of ecstasy over and over again, and from that night on she had been completely addicted to the man. She had been madly in love, and willingly she had followed where he'd led. With hindsight she realised she should have guessed then for Lucas it had only been sex. She felt a deep ache in the region of her heart, and gritted her teeth. She hadn't expected the memory to hurt so much...

Lucas walked past her, discarding his jacket and tie on a low velvet-covered sofa, and headed straight for the drinks trolley. 'What will you have?' he asked, and only then did she lift her head and glance at him.

'Nothing,' she croaked. With his shirt half open and a tantalising glimpse of silky black chest hair exposed and his pleated trousers resting snugly on his slim hips, he looked exactly as he had all those years ago.

One ebony brow rose enquiringly. 'You must, I insist.'

'No, I'm driving later.' She swallowed hard and looked away. 'A fruit juice, maybe,' she amended.

A moment later Lucas was handing her a glass of orange juice. She took it with a steady hand but made sure her fingers did not come into contact with his.

'You look hot,' he opined, his dark eyes searching on her flushed face. 'Let me take your jacket.'

'No, no.' With a glass of juice in one hand and her briefcase in the other, there was no way she could remove it, and he certainly wasn't going to. She had no faith in the fine silk of her blouse hiding her body's reaction to his intimidating male presence.

'Please yourself, but at least let me take this.' And before she could react, his large hand prised her fingers from the death-like grip she had on her briefcase. 'We are eating on the terrace. Are you sure I can't persuade you out of your jacket? It is a warm night.'

Warm did not begin to describe how Amber was suddenly feeling and she almost fell over her feet to rush out onto the terrace, and take a great gulp of air.

A moment later Lucas followed her out with a glass of whisky in one hand, and, casting a sardonic glance at her stiff body standing by the balustrade, he pulled out a chair at the perfectly set table.

'For heaven's sake! Sit down and relax, Amber. I'm not about to jump you.'

'I never thought you were,' she responded with admirable poise and took the seat he offered.

Surprisingly Amber enjoyed the meal, probably because she had hardly eaten any lunch, but also because Lucas was at his charming best. Not a hint of innuendo, or mention of the past. The conversation was topical; some politics, the latest show to open in the West End, which Amber had seen, Lucas had not.

'I didn't know you liked the theatre,' Lucas remarked. 'I never thought to take you when we were together.'

Sitting back in her chair, sipping at a cup of black coffee, Amber almost choked. He was back to personal and she did not like it. 'You never took me anywhere,' she said flatly, draining her cup.

'You're right. Except to bed, of course, as I recall we had the greatest difficulty leaving the bedroom.'

Hot colour flooded her face but Amber wasn't touching that one with a bargepole. 'Shall we stick to business? I meant what I said earlier—whatever Spiro has left me, you can have. I know the will must have been an oversight on his part, or laziness. Either way you are the rightful heir. I don't see any problem.'

'Even if I believed your offer, there are several huge obstacles,' Lucas intoned cynically. 'Never mind the death duty, which will be quite substantial, his medical bills are enormous.'

'Did he die of Aids?' Amber asked, but she'd already guessed the answer.

'Of course, after a protracted illness,' Lucas stated flatly. 'I gather you have not had much contact with Spiro.'

'I hadn't spoken to him in four years,' she said, nervously fingering the waist button on her jacket and slipping it open. She felt terribly guilty, though she knew deep down it wasn't rational. Spiro had been a law unto himself.

'Okay. In that case I'd better fill you in.'

For a brief second she imagined his long body, naked, literally doing just that, and to her horror her own body betrayed her, a wave of heat washing over the surface of her skin, her breasts swelling against the constraint of her bra. Thankfully Lucas did not seem to be aware of the effect his simple statement had aroused.

'Well, you know Spiro,' Lucas prompted, exasperation lacing his tone. 'From taking control of his inheritance, he spent money like a madman. He bought most of the pictures in his art gallery from the artists himself. "Friends", he called them. For the last few years he has hired a house on Fire Island every summer, apparently a very popular place with the gay community, and he always took a crowd of pals along to share it with him. He sold off twenty per cent of his share of Karadines without my knowledge. I don't think he did it deliberately to harm the company, but it didn't help. He needed money fast and a friend fixed it for him.'

'How so Spiro,' Amber groaned with feeling. 'Even in death he caused chaos.'

'You knew him well,' Lucas commented dryly. 'But settling up after my father and Christina has left me with a bit of a cash-flow problem. I haven't got the capital to buy Spiro's shares at the moment—but if I don't own them, the company will be very vulnerable to predators.'

And he should know, Amber silently concluded. Lucas was the biggest predator she knew. She glanced across at him, her golden eyes narrowing shrewdly on his darkly attractive face. That was it! Amber saw the flaw in his argument. Lucas *should* know the solution. He had a brilliant brain and was a sharp operator of worldwide renown. He was also wickedly sexy with his shirt unbuttoned, came the unbidden thought. Stop it, Amber. Concentrate, she told herself firmly. Lucas was up to something, but what?

'But why can't I just give you Spiro's share?' she asked, feeling her way.

'I have never taken money off a woman in my life and I am not going to start now. I will buy your shares, eventually.'

'When you're over your cash-flow problems.'

He nodded. His eyes were hooded, masking his expression. Hers were hopefully blandly business-like. The treacherous thought did flicker through her mind that she was in the perfect position to exact a devastating revenge on the man who had thought of her as little better than a slut, a sex object to be used and discarded when he felt like it. For a fleeting moment she let her mind dwell on the idea of selling to another party. It was no more than Lucas Karadines deserved; her lips curved in a wry smile. But she knew she couldn't do it...

Rising abruptly from the table, Lucas said, 'It is getting distinctly chilly out here, we can carry on our discussion inside.'

Amber's mouth opened to deny him, but, catching the cynical expression on his handsome face, she thought better of it. She had the distinct impression he had read her mind and was not talking about the weather at all.

Rising, she followed him back into the sitting room, and, carefully positioning herself on the edge of an armchair, she refused his offer of a brandy. She simply watched and waited.

'My solution...' having poured himself a generous helping of brandy into a crystal goblet, Lucas turned and walked towards her...'is as I said earlier today... You and I, Amber, are now the major partners in Karadines. As you have probably worked out, you can make life very difficult for me, and I could hardly blame you, after the way I treated you.'

His answer floored her. He actually sounded contrite. Her golden eyes widened to their fullest extent on his, and he smiled down at her, a small smile, but a smile nevertheless.

'Don't look so surprised.' His gaze narrowed and swept over her tensely held body perched on the end of the chair,

lingering at where her breasts were outlined beneath the
fine silk of her blouse. She had forgotten she had undone
her jacket. 'The past four years have taught me that love
is an illusion and what we shared was a lot more honest
emotion.'

Amber gulped, and jumped to her feet. No way was she
going there! And, fastening the button of her jacket, 'This
is all very interesting but I really must be going. And if
you want my advice...' she said briskly, spying her briefcase leaning against the end of the sofa and she headed
towards it. Picking it up, she turned and finally glanced
up at Lucas. 'I'm a stockbroker—if you need to raise
money, float the company on the stock market.'

'Come now, Amber,' he drawled mockingly. 'Do you
really think that I, Lucas Karadines, would ever give up
control of Karadines?'

His impregnable confidence made her suddenly angry;
her golden eyes flashed. 'You might have to.'

'Not if you agree to my plan, Amber,' he murmured,
his glance intent on her lovely face as he towered over
her. 'If you are as honest as you say, you know Spiro
would never have intended the family firm to fall into
other hands or even collapse.'

Lucas was right. Spiro used to rant and rave about his
family, but deep down he had cared for them. Amber's
golden gaze studied Lucas, and her pulses raced. She'd
been struggling to keep her eyes off him all evening, the
tempting view of his near-naked chest, and with only
inches separating them she knew she had to get away.

'What exactly is your plan?' she asked abruptly. She
would listen to him, agree and get out fast.

'It's quite simple,' he murmured. His black eyes lingered on her high cheekbones, the thick, curling lashes
framing her wide-set golden eyes, and then lower to the

full curve of her lips, and lower still to the soft swell of her breast.

'Get on with it,' Amber prompted, terrified by the latent sensual gleam in his dark eyes.

He was too close. Far, far too close. 'Just—just *tell* me,' she stammered, somewhat breathlessly. *Turn, run,* her mind screamed. But she had waited too long.

Lucas hauled her hard against him, his dark head swooped down and his mouth closed over hers. Amber gasped, and his tongue gained instant access to the moist, dark interior of her mouth. Her briefcase fell from her hand and clattered to the floor. But Amber was unconscious of the fact. She was only aware of the hard heat of Lucas, the rock-like strength of his arousal pressed against her lower body, the greedy hunger of his mouth as he ravished hers, and her own instant fierce response.

His hands slid down from her shoulders, and she lifted her own to clasp them around his neck. She clung to him, as one large hand delved down the front of her blouse to cup the soft curve of her breast, long fingers slipping under the strip of lace that was her bra. Amber shuddered as he flicked a nail over a nipple, bringing it to a rigid, pulsing peak. With his other hand closed over her bottom, she instinctively rotated her hips sensually against his hard thighs, wanting more.

Lucas lifted his head, his breath hot against her cheek, and watched her with night-black eyes. 'You haven't changed,' he said huskily with an edge of triumph in his tone. 'Still the sexiest girl alive.' His lips caressed hers softly.

Amber stiffened, her hands fell from his neck, and she turned her head away from his searching mouth. He was right, damn him... Nothing had changed in the intervening years, she realized. She was still helplessly enslaved to the potent sexuality of this one man… But she was older and wiser…and, fighting for every bit of will-power, she flattened both hands on his chest and pushed.

'Let me go,' she demanded bitterly. She could feel the heavy pounding of his heart beneath her hand, the angry tension in his body. She lifted her eyes to his, and caught a flash of something violent that quickly vanished.

'As you wish, Amber.' He threw his arms wide and stepped back. 'I have discovered all I needed to know.' His dark eyes had a glitter in them, and more than a hint of triumph.

Amber gazed at him, her eyes clouded with puzzlement and the lingering traces of passion. To hide her confusion, she bent down and retrieved her briefcase, and, straightening up, she smoothed her jacket down over the curve of her hips with a trembling hand. 'If you want my co-operation over Spiro's legacy, you can cut that out for a start,' she said icily. 'Otherwise you can sort Karadines' problems out yourself. I'm sure you're more than capable.' She headed for the door.

'I am.' Lucas smiled, catching her wrist and spinning her back to face him. 'The solution is simple: I marry you,' he declared, a hint of satisfaction in his voice. 'You did ask me once before, remember?' He taunted softly.

Amber would have given everything she owned not to. Her face went ashen, the passion and the pain inextricably linked in her mind. She had swallowed her pride and begged him to love her. Until finally he had told her the truth—that she disgusted him.

'Over my dead body.' Wrenching her wrist from his grasp, she looked at him with loathing in her eyes. 'My God! Your arrogance is only exceeded by your colossal conceit in daring to ask the question.'

'I did not ask a question.' His black eyes glinted mockingly. 'I made a statement of intent.'

CHAPTER SEVEN

As AMBER tried to find her voice through the anger that consumed her she told herself, He has to be joking! But Lucas did not look particularly amused. In fact, the cold determination in his black eyes sent an icy shiver of fear slithering down her spine. 'I don't have to listen to this,' she declared forcibly. 'I'm leaving.'

'No, you are not,' Lucas countered coolly, and slipped an arm around her waist, drawing her ruthlessly closer. She felt the heat of him searing her even through her clothes. Amber's lips went dry, her throat closing in panic. Lucas was holding her tightly. She tried to struggle free, but he simply increased the pressure, crushing her to the hardness of his body. 'I have no intention of letting you go,' he muttered, 'ever again.' He grasped her chin with one large hand and tilted her head back. 'Look at me!' he commanded.

She wanted to escape, and planted her hands firmly on his chest intending to push him away, but the old familiar sexual chemistry held her in thrall, and had he actually said 'ever again'? The notion was beguiling and the best she could do was stare up at him with puzzled, angry eyes.

Her anger seemed to amuse him, and as his dark gaze bored into her she felt the surge of blood in her cheeks, and began to tremble, her legs suddenly weak as with a faint, mocking smile he told her exactly what he wanted.

'You and I will marry a week on Saturday in Greece.' His fingers traced up over her lips in intentional provocation. 'I can take you to bed now, and remind you how it was with us, or we can wait for the wedding. But that is the only choice I'm giving you.'

Amber knew she should be fighting him, but could only gaze at him in shock, with increasing need and desire scorching through her. 'No,' she denied. But his mouth found hers, deriding her negative with a demanding hunger that had her weakening helplessly against him. With sensual expertise he deepened the kiss until a drugging passion had emptied her mind of everything but a growing physical need, an ache she had to have assuaged.

He was using the potent force of his sexuality to get his own way, and even as she recognised the fact Amber suddenly did not care! A wild recklessness filled her, sweeping away the years since Lucas had held her like this, kissed her like this, and, slipping her hands over his chest, she clasped them behind his neck, pressing her slender body to his mighty frame. It was only when he broke the kiss and held her slightly away from him, his breathing ragged, she realised the full extent of her capitulation.

'Come to bed with me, you know you want to.' His dark eyes blazed with triumph; he had sensed her complete surrender and taken it as a yes, now he was simply discussing the terms. 'Now or next week, what does it matter?'

Amber would have denied him, even as her body was on fire for him. His assumption he only had to kiss her and she would give in was an insult to her pride, her self-esteem. But then he groaned.

'*Christo!* I certainly need you.' The hand at her chin was suddenly gentle, and he stared deep into her golden eyes. 'Say yes.' She gulped at the unguarded hunger, the desire she saw in expressive eyes. 'I'll wait for the wedding night if you insist,' he said, his smile almost tender.

It was the tenderness that did it. She wanted him. Oh!

How she wanted him, and why not? her sex-starved body demanded. She was not going to marry him, she was no longer a lovesick girl, or a fool, but with every nerve in her body screaming with frustration she murmured, 'All right.' At least she could have this one night.

Lucas smiled, a slow, sensual twist, then raised his hands to her head and deftly unpinned the severe chignon, and trailed his fingers through the long length of her hair, spreading it over her shoulders. Eyes closed, Amber trembled as his arm slid down around her waist and he rested his head in the curve of her neck, breathing in the fragrant scent of the tumbling mass of hair.

'I have been longing to do this,' he murmured. 'From the second I walked into your office today and saw your magnificent hair scraped back, my fingers ached to set it free. It should always be free.' His lips moving over her burning cheek finally found her mouth.

The years since they had last met might never have been. Her pulse leapt as Lucas kissed her with a wild, yet tender, passion she was helpless to deny. She didn't want to. She felt the sudden rush of damp heat flooding her lower body, and feverishly she clung to him, silently abandoning herself to the sheer ecstasy of his kiss, his touch.

Swiftly Lucas swept her up in his arms. She put her arms around his neck and she kissed him very slowly and long. Amber wasn't really conscious of him lowering her to her feet and removing their clothing as desire mounted fiercely inside her. She touched a slender finger to his lips, remembering, tracing the firm outline—he had such a sensual mouth. Lucas drew a ragged breath, and urged her down onto the bed. She felt the mattress at her back, and stared up at him with passion-glazed eyes. He was magnificent in his nudity; his shoulders were broad, his hips were narrow and his belly flat and hard, and the awesome sight of his aroused manhood made her shudder in almost fearful anticipation.

For a long, tense moment Lucas looked down at her, drinking in her naked beauty with black hungry eyes, then, leaning over, he kissed her, his mouth possessive and urgent on her own.

Then, rearing back, he touched her and she quivered like a leaf in the breeze. His hands swept slowly down her body in a long, sinuous, almost worshipful motion, then up again, his palms flat on her stomach until they reached her breasts. He teased her gently, the fingers of one hand grazing slowly over the tips of her breasts, first one and then the other, bringing them to rigid, aching peaks, while his other hand smoothed back down between her legs that parted involuntarily at his caress. She was moist, ready, aching for him, and with a delicate, erotic touch he caressed her until desire mounted crazily inside her and everything else was blotted from her mind.

He caught her to him, and their mouths met and fused, and she arched herself blindly against him. With tactile delight she slipped her hands down across his shoulders, and along under his arms, across his taut abdomen, and then they swept around the outside of his thighs and finally to his inner thigh, her slender fingers curving around the hard, pulsing strength of him. She wanted him now...

She heard the sharp intake of his breath as his head tilted back. 'No, Amber.' And he closed his hand over hers, pulling it from his body. For a horrible second she thought he meant to deny her. 'Not yet. I was a brute the last time,' he rasped. 'I vowed...'

She could see the muscles of his thighs bunch with tension in the effort of control. But after five years of celibacy Amber didn't want to talk. So she wrapped her arms around his neck, and pulled him back down over her.

He kissed her with a wild hunger, his tongue exploring deep in her mouth, his hands caressing every inch of her burning flesh with sensual delight, and she responded with equal passion and helpless moans of pleasure.

She sank back under his hard, hot body, whimpering with need. But Lucas was not to be hurried. He kissed her mouth, her breasts, her thighs, until she jerked helplessly beneath him, her senses swimming with desire. 'Please, Lucas, don't make me wait,' she begged.

And as though he'd been waiting for her plea Lucas moved between her parted thighs. Amber tensed for a second. It had been a long time for her. The hard length of him moved slowly, easing himself deeper and deeper inside her, sometimes to his full length and sometimes with shallow strokes that teased and enhanced the pleasure almost to pain. Amber had never felt such need, such fiery tension, until her inner muscles convulsed around him in a shattering completion. But still he moved, their bodies locked together.

Lucas rolled onto his back and brought her up above him. His hands clasping her hips, he held her against him, but now he could kiss her breasts. Amber cried out at the feel of his mouth on her taut nipples, and shockingly felt the excitement building all over again.

'Yes, yes,' Lucas cried, and as he held her fiercely down on him his great body bucked violently beneath her as he reached his climax. At the same time Amber cried his name, and tumbled over into her own headlong fulfilment yet again.

She collapsed on top of him, breathless and mindless, feeling the sweat of passion cooling on her skin. She buried her head on his shoulder. She did not want him to see her, not yet. Not until she had recovered some of her shattered control. She felt his large, warm hand stroke her back gently, and she could almost fool herself it was love... But not quite...

Rolling off him, she lay flat on her back, and swallowed a despairing sigh—from the heights of ecstasy to the depths of despair in a few moments. Amber knew herself well—no way would she allow any man the intimate liberties she had gloried in with Lucas unless she loved him. The enormity of the realisation made her heartsick.

She loved him, she always had and probably always would. But she had been too badly hurt before to believe he wanted to marry her for any other reason than Spiro's legacy. Tonight would have to be enough. It was ironic in a way, she thought as a wry smile curved her love-swollen lips. Lucas had called her a gold-digger, but in fact it was Lucas who was now in that position.

'What are you thinking?' Lucas propped himself on one elbow, his dark, slumberous eyes boring into hers, his breathing still unsteady. 'That smile looks decidedly smug.'

It was a question she did not want to answer, not truthfully. The night was young and she intended to make full use of it. She lifted her hands and trailed her fingers through the silky mat of chest hair, caressing his body. As her finger grazed a hard male nipple she felt his magnificent body tremble, and she smiled again. 'I was wondering how long it takes you to recover these days,' she murmured throatily, her eyes gleaming with invitation.

Surreptitiously Amber glanced at her wrist-watch—it was the only thing she was wearing. It was close to one o'clock in the morning. She looked down into the face of Lucas Karadines. Somehow he seemed much younger in sleep. His eyes were closed, his long dark lashes brushing his cheeks. He was deeply asleep, not surprising after their second encounter, Amber thought, remembering his seemingly insatiable desire. But she could not sleep—she had to leave. Even now, with her passion for him momentarily quenched, she felt no lessening of desire, but she knew on Lucas's part it was only lust… He had told her so quite truthfully years ago. Dear heaven! What was it going to take for her to get over him? Death?

On that morbid thought she stifled a sigh and slid out of bed, and by moonlight she managed to find her clothes and get dressed. Slipping her shoes on, she crept quietly towards the door. She turned for one last look at his bronzed body spread out on the bed, and almost went back to join him. Instead she closed the door on the temptation he provided.

She didn't get far! Finding her jacket on the arm of the sofa, she slipped it on, and, picking up her briefcase, she stepped towards the exit and escape, just when the bedroom door was flung open.

'Amber.' Lucas walked into the sitting room, totally unconscious of his nudity. 'What are you doing?'

'I am leaving.'

Lucas glared at her for a startled second. 'What the hell is wrong with you? Are you out of your mind? We have just shared mind-blowing sex and now you are sneaking out of my bed in the middle of the night!'

Pushing the tangled mass of her hair behind her ears in a futile attempt to tame it, she glanced up at Lucas. He had the angry, puzzled look of a child who had had his favourite toy snatched from his grasp, and his crude comment on sex simply angered her further. 'Why, was I supposed to wait until you left first?' she asked cynically.

If tonight had taught her anything at all, it was that she had to stay away from Lucas. Because, loving him as she did, she had no resistance against him; she was his for the

taking. Even now the temptation to close the distance between them and run her hands over his hard, tanned body,
to feel once more the wonder of his possession, was almost
irresistible. But one thought stopped her. The memory of
his leaving her naked on the floor in the apartment they
had once shared was something she would not let herself
forget. She moved to walk past him, but his hand shot out
and he captured her arm in a steely grip.

'I have no intention of leaving you—' he glared down
at her pale face and bruised, swollen mouth '—or of letting
you go. You belong to me!'

'Spiro's money belongs to you is what you really
mean.'

He frowned at her acid comment. 'If that is what you
want to think, so be it. But it does not alter the fact you
are marrying me. I had hoped willingly.' His black eyes
raked appreciatively over her. 'You're a very beautiful,
intelligent woman; any man would be proud to make you
his wife.'

A harsh laugh escaped her. 'Oh, please, Lucas,' she
drawled scathingly, tugging her arm free and stepping
back. 'It's a bit late for compliments.' Five years too late,
she thought bitterly.

His dark eyes blazed angrily for a second before adopt-
ing his more usual expression, coldly remote. 'If you say
so.' He shrugged his broad shoulders. 'But if not willingly,
I am quite prepared to use coercion. The end result will
be the same.'

He sounded so uncompromising that Amber flinched.
'But why?' she demanded in exasperation, trying not to
look at his naked body. 'I have told you to contact my
lawyer. I will put it in writing here and now, if you like.
You can have the lot.' Her temper was frayed, she was
tired and beginning to be afraid. There was something

about his insistence on marriage that was finally getting through to her. He was deadly serious.

'Because of the time-scale, Amber, even if I believe your assurance that you don't want Spiro's legacy, I don't want you to give it to me,' he insisted for the second time, much to Amber's puzzlement. 'I will pay you the going rate for your holding. But first there is the small question of probate. It usually takes months for a will to get through, and in the meantime the company will become vulnerable to rumour as to how you intend to disperse Spiro's shares,' Lucas answered grimly. 'You will be inundated with offers, and, much as I want to believe in your altruistic nature, I prefer to make sure. As my wife it will be apparent to any predator the company is being kept firmly in the family.'

Amber had enough business sense to realise there was a flaw in his argument. 'In that case the answer is simple. I will give you first option to buy the shares at a knock-down price when I finally inherit. Problem solved,' she said jauntily.

'I prefer my solution. We both know there is the possibility of you marrying Clive Thompson—' he almost spat the name out '—and there is no way he is getting anywhere near my business.' Lucas's glittering glance was full of macho rage. He knew Amber would not be easy to fool, she was too damn smart. But after the great sex they had shared there was no way on God's earth he was letting her get away again. He had spent far too many long, lonely nights frustrated as hell. He looked grimly down at her. 'And if you have any fondness for your new-found father and family, you will do as I say.'

To Amber's ears that sounded suspiciously like a threat. A terrible coldness invaded her and, cautiously lifting her head, she looked into his jet-black eyes. 'What exactly do you mean by that?' she demanded quietly.

'Wait here while I dress,' Lucas commanded and strode back into the bedroom, leaving Amber standing in an agony of suspense. She considered walking out, but didn't dare. Lucas had been so chillingly confident, she had to know what he meant.

When he returned, Amber's wary gaze swept over him. He looked casually elegant. Light-coloured linen trousers hung easily on his lean hips, a fine knit roll-neck sweater covered his muscular chest and his black hair was brushed firmly from his broad brow. 'Good, you waited. I rather thought you might,' he stated silkily. 'Now, where were we?' he asked, smiling.

She felt like knocking the grin off his face, but instead gathered all the will-power she possessed and took a couple of steadying breaths. 'You were about to tell me why I should not marry Clive but marry you instead. Personally I thought it was my own choice. How silly of me,' she managed to say facetiously.

Lucas's smile vanished. 'You have no choice.' His dark eyes narrowed to angry slits. 'Not if you value your father's good name.' Amber felt a sick feeling in the pit of her stomach as Lucas continued. 'Since Sir David retired, his bank has not, how shall I put it…?' He hesitated; his black eyes, glittering with triumph, clashed with hers. 'His son Mark is not a patch on him. Last year, although it saddened me to do it given the long association between Karadines and Janson's, I had to cut all ties with the bank. It was only out of deference for Sir David that charges were not brought against them.'

'I don't believe you,' Amber said sharply. 'My father is an honest man.'

'Yes, I agree. Unfortunately the same cannot be said for his son,' Lucas opined cynically.

Amber went white, and in a voice that shook she asked, 'You're telling me that Mark has done something illegal?' The horrible part was, Amber realized that she was not completely surprised by Lucas's statement.

Lucas shot her a caustic smile. 'What else would you call using money from a client's account to fund a yacht in the Med and keeping a very expensive mistress?'

Amber turned her head aside, unable to meet his eyes. Mark had bought a yacht, that much was true, and the mistress didn't surprise her much either. His poor wife Mary was the mother of three delightful daughters, and spent her whole time apologising for not producing the son her husband wanted.

Lucas walked over to her, his long fingers clasping her chin. 'If you don't believe me, ask him, Amber,' he challenged.

She had a terrible feeling Lucas might be right, and she hid her confusion with an angry accusation. 'You would use the feeling I have for my father to blackmail me into marrying you?' she derided. 'In your dreams, buster.'

His jaw tensed and something violent flashed in his eyes before he drew a deep breath. 'Not in a dream, but in reality, yes. If that's what it takes to get what I want. Yes,' he reiterated bluntly.

She searched his lean, strong face, sure he must be kidding. Surely no man in the twenty-first century could force a woman into marriage? He didn't mean it. But she could not help noticing the implacable determination in his gaze. How had she forgotten what a ruthless bastard he could be? She'd fooled herself into thinking she could have him for a night and walk away. Amber felt her stomach curl sickeningly with fear as her eyes skimmed over his mag-

nificent physique, the vibrant raw energy of the man that
fascinated her even as it repelled her. She had underesti-
mated Lucas. But she'd also overestimated her own ability
to control her chaotic emotions. Her eyes widened in horror. 'You're crazy,' she bit out as realisation dawned. He
was serious, and, worse, much worse, she was tempted...

One ebony brow lifted while a ruthless smile curved his
sensuous mouth. 'Perhaps, but how would you live with
yourself knowing you could have saved the reputation of
your father's firm? A father who went to great lengths to
find you and acknowledge you.'

She was trembling. 'You're a bastard, Lucas,' she said,
her strained features reflecting her inner turmoil. 'But I'm
not afraid of you. I will ask Mark, and—'

He cut across her. 'You *do* that. I made my decision a
while ago, I'll give you until the day after tomorrow to
make yours.'

Amber heard the car drive up, the engine stop and the car
door slam. Her full lips tightened in an angry grimace as
she glanced out of the window of her living room. Lucas
was pushing open the wrought-iron gate that led up the
garden path to the front door of her cottage.

Since the night when she'd fallen like a ripe plum into
his arms, in his hotel suite, her life had become chaotic.
The following evening she'd met Mark, her half-brother,
for a drink, and as soon as she'd mentioned Lucas
Karadines he had gone white, and within minutes she'd
had the whole story: it was true. It would have been risible
if the consequences had not been so tragic for Amber.

Wednesday morning Lucas had called at her office.
Loyalty to her father's family and her guilty feelings over
Spiro's legacy had forced her to accept Lucas's proposal.
Because she knew she did not deserve to gain by Spiro's

death. He had been a good friend for many years, as a student and after. Yet she had not contacted him in over four years because he had invited his uncle to the opening of his art gallery without telling her, and told Lucas that she'd put up the capital for Spiro's venture. Worse, she could not shake the notion that if she had not given Spiro the money to go to New York when he had, he might not have contracted the disease that had killed him. But the fact that Lucas the devil had won did nothing to soothe her anger.

That weekend, at Lucas's insistence, she had taken him to her father's house in Surrey, and dropped the bombshell of her forthcoming marriage the following Saturday. Lucas had charmed Sir David and his wife Mildred so much so that Mildred had insisted on throwing an engagement party. Amber had been glad to get back to work on the Monday and away from Lucas, who had business in New York for a few days. But then she'd had the unenviable task of lunching with Clive and telling him she was marrying Lucas Karadines. She had felt an absolute worm by the time they had parted, because she hadn't been able to tell Clive the real reason for her hasty marriage, and he'd taken her rejection with a brave smile and an honest desire that they remain friends.

Then mid-week she'd discovered Lucas had spoken to the chairman of Brentford's. The firm had given her three months' holiday. When she had discovered from one of the other partners why, she had been furious and deeply hurt in equal proportions.

She heard the doorbell ring. They were flying out to Greece today and tomorrow was their wedding day. 'Unfortunately,' Amber muttered darkly, smoothing the fine buttercup silk summer dress she had chosen to wear over her slender hips, and, taking a deep, calming breath, she walked out of the living room, along the hall and opened the front door.

Lucas stood on the path, tall and dark, and the expression on his strong face was one of amusement. 'I don't believe it—you live in a country cottage with roses around the door. It is not you at all, Amber,' he drawled mockingly.

Put out by his opening comment, Amber snapped, 'How the hell would you know?' Her heart had leapt at the sight of him—she had not seen him since last Sunday.

A green polo shirt fit snugly over his wide shoulders, and outlined the musculature of his broad chest in loving detail. Khaki cotton trousers clung to his hips and long legs. A pair of sunglasses was shoved carelessly back across the thick black hair of his head, revealing his perfect features in stark beauty. It wasn't fair; no man should look so good. Even the summer sun glinting on the silver wings of his hair only enhanced his vibrant masculine charm.

Lucas straightened. 'As I recall I know you very well.' His dark eyes roamed over her face and down over her shapely figure in a blatant sensual caress.

'Only in the biblical sense,' Amber returned, and, turning back into the hall, she grabbed the case she had packed and walked to the door. 'I'm ready. Let's go.' She did not want to invite him into her home, because she knew her marriage to Lucas would only last as long as it took Spiro's will to pass probate. She loved her cottage; she had bought it from her landlord three years ago, and had had great fun renovating it. She wanted no memories of Lucas to haunt it when she returned.

'Is that all your luggage?' Lucas demanded, one dark brow arching incredulously on the single suitcase. 'We are getting married in the morning, we will be in Greece for at least the rest of the summer. Where are all your clothes? Surely not in that thing.' He flung an elegant tanned hand at her admittedly rather battered suitcase.

'Let's get one thing straight here, Lucas. I don't need anything special for a civil marriage that is strictly business and will be terminated as soon as possible; the dress I am wearing will do. Easy-care wash and dry as are the other clothes I have packed. I don't need much to bum around on a Greek beach for three months, which is *all* I will be doing since you took it upon yourself to get my employer to give me a holiday. Understood?' Amber told him belligerently, squaring up to him, her golden eyes flashing. If he thought for one second she was going to socialise with him, or play the part of the loving wife, or climb into his bed like a good little girl, he was in for a rude awakening.

Black eyes clashed with hers, and she saw the glint of fury before he successfully masked it with self-restraint.

'Amber, you can walk around naked, if that is what you want,' he drawled mockingly. 'In fact, I would prefer you to.' His eyes, flaring with sensual heat, roamed over her body. She looked breathtakingly beautiful, the buttercup silk dress outlining her luscious curves in loving detail. Her eyes were wide and lustrous, with just a trace of vulnerability in their golden depths that her anger could not hide. She was nowhere near as confident as she wanted to appear.

'Oh, that is not what I mean and you know it,' she snapped.

Lucas knew now was not the time to argue. 'It was a joke, Amber, I hear what you are saying. A business arrangement.'

Expecting an argument, Amber was surprised at his easy agreement, and for a moment felt ridiculously disappointed. But then what had she expected? She remonstrated with her foolish heart. Lucas had not wanted her five years ago, he was hardly going to be desperate to marry her now. On that sobering thought she brushed past him, dropped the suitcase on the path, and turned to lock the door of her little cottage.

'What exactly do you intend doing with this place?' Lucas asked, picking up her suitcase in one hand, his other hand settling at the base of her rigid spine as he urged her away from the house.

'Why, nothing,' she informed him dulcetly. 'I expect to be back at work in three months.' Lucas wasn't getting it all his own way. He had ridden roughshod over all her objections, charmed her father, and bribed her boss to give her a three-month sabbatical, by the simple expedient of becoming a client of Brentford's. He might have blackmailed her into marriage, but he was definitely not blackmailing her into his bed again.

'Well, it is a bit small, but I suppose I could get used to it,' Lucas murmured.

Amber tensed. 'What do you mean by that?'

His sensuous mouth tilted at the corners. 'Why, Amber, darling, once we are married, what is mine is yours, and what is yours is mine.'

Amber's eyes widened in astonishment at his words. 'You're joking.'

'If you want us to live in a cottage rather than a mansion,' he said, shrugging his broad shoulders. His dark eyes watched the myriad expressions flicker across her exquisite face, and then flicked appreciatively over the soft curve of her breasts, the narrow waist and on down over the slender hips and long legs. 'I don't mind,' Lucas said huskily, his dark eyes dancing wickedly.

He was laughing at her; she should have been furious.

'But—but, I—I mean you have just agreed the marriage is strictly business,' Amber stammered to a halt. He was handsome, a rampantly virile male, and she stared at him, her breath catching in her throat.

'I know *exactly* what you mean, Amber,' Lucas emphasised dryly. 'You are angling for a fight and I flatly refuse to give you one. Business marriage or whatever! If my competitors are to be convinced, we have to live together for as long as it takes. Now relax, the sun is shining, it is a beautiful day, and tomorrow will be even better. Get in the car and let's go.' With a broad grin he urged her out onto the road and into the passenger seat of a black BMW.

She watched him through lowered lashes as he slid into the driving seat after depositing her suitcase in the back. Why had she even imagined for a moment that she would be able to resist Lucas, deny him her body? If he wanted her he only had to smile at her, and she was lost. Why had she even tried to pretend she hated him? She loved him, and the realisation of exactly how vulnerable she was hurt like hell. But it made her all the more determined to defy him.

Starting the car, Lucas turned his dark head and smiled at her again. 'I have a surprise for you when we get to the airport.'

Her own vulnerability to his blatant masculine charm made her respond with biting sarcasm. 'Let's hope it is the same surprise as the last time you said that to me. You are marrying someone else...'

Lucas stiffened, his smile vanishing, his dark eyes staring straight ahead, watching the road. Amber noticed the dull stain of red on his cheekbones and for a second thought he was embarrassed until he spoke. 'No, this time it has to be you. I have no choice.'

Amber opened her mouth to argue and stopped. Shrinking back in the seat, she let her thoughts loose, and winced at her own conceit. She had been so incensed at being conned into marrying Lucas, convinced she was making a great sacrifice for her family; she had never thought for a moment how Lucas had to feel. He had loved his first wife, Christina, and now because of Spiro's will he was stuck with either trusting Amber, or marrying her. His only other alternative was facing a takeover battle for his business.

A very chastened Amber said, 'It is not too late. We don't have to marry. You can trust me to give you Spiro's legacy, Lucas. I won't betray you.'

A large tanned hand dropped from the wheel to curve over her thigh. Involuntarily her leg flexed, electric sensation tingling down to her toes. Lucas shot her a deep and unfathomable look.

'Sorry, Amber,' he said softly, 'but I do have to marry you.' With a brief squeeze of her leg, he returned his hand to the steering wheel.

With her thigh still burning from his touch, she couldn't think of a thing to say. She closed her eyes to be alone with her thoughts. He had said sorry. Did he mean he was sorry for her? Or sorry for himself because he had to marry her?

Trying to fathom out how Lucas's mind worked was doing her head in, and, opening her eyes, she looked out of the passenger window and realised they were approaching the airport.

CHAPTER EIGHT

'SO WHAT is the mysterious surprise?' Amber finally demanded. The long silence, the heightened tension in the close confines of the car, had her nerves stretched to breaking-point.

'You will soon find out,' Lucas said curtly, bringing the car to a halt at the entrance to the airport terminal and, without so much as looking in her direction, he proceeded to unfasten his seat belt. Whatever the surprise was, Lucas obviously had no intention of enlightening her.

'Get out.' The terse command did nothing for Amber's growing resentment at his high-handed manner. She cast him a fulminating glance but it was wasted as he was already sliding out of the driver's seat, his back towards her.

Amber scrambled out of the car with more haste than elegance, and, straightening up, she flicked her mane of chestnut hair back from her shoulders and looked around.

Lucas stood a couple of feet away. She watched as he lifted an elegant tanned hand and, magically, a small, rather wizened man appeared and caught the car key Lucas threw in his direction. The older man looked vaguely familiar to Amber and, walking forward, she stopped at Lucas's side as the strange man withdrew her suitcase from the car, handed it to Lucas and said something in Greek.

Watching Lucas respond in the same language and smile down at the other man, Amber was diverted from her simmering anger by trying to figure out where she had seen him before. Then the old man lifted his head, grinned at her and she remembered.

'Why, it's you,' the asinine comment slipped out, but the man had turned and was already getting into the car. 'That's the man that called at the apartment,' Amber said impulsively, tilting her head to look up at Lucas. 'I remember him.' She beamed, pleased at having placed the stranger.

One dark brow arched sardonically as their eyes met. 'Ah, yes! The symbolic castration! I don't think a trip down that particular memory lane is appropriate, given we are to be married tomorrow,' Lucas drawled cynically.

Instinctively her eyes dropped to a certain part of his anatomy; realising what she was doing, she quickly glanced back up at his face. 'No. No...' she stammered. She had forgotten her vengeful reaction when she'd destroyed the crotch in his trousers, and felt colour burn up through her skin. Through anger, she decided staunchly, not embarrassment.

The look he cast her held a tinge of amusement that was apparent in his voice. 'It was probably no more than I deserved, given the circumstances. Forget it—I have—and give me your passport, we have to get a move on.'

Whether it was embarrassment, anger, or sheer shock that Lucas had actually admitted he might have been at fault, which was surely a first for the great Lucas Karadines, it did not matter. Amber was flustered enough to delve into her bag, withdraw her passport and hand it to him without a murmur.

'Good girl.' And, cupping a large hand around her elbow, he led her through the airport.

Following his broad back up the steps to the aircraft, Amber fumed at the sheer arrogant confidence of Lucas. He had swept them both through customs, with an ease that lesser mortals could never aspire to. She watched him smile at the stewardess waiting at the entrance door to the plane, and saw the stupid girl simpering all over him. By the time Amber reached the door, the same girl simply bared her teeth at Amber.

Walking into the cabin, Amber stopped dead.

'Surprise, surprise,' a cacophony of voices shouted.

Amber's mouth fell open in shock, her golden eyes widening to their fullest extent. Everyone and their granny were on the aircraft, she registered in stunned amazement.

Lucas stepped forward to curve a confident arm around her rigid body. 'This is your surprise...I thought you would appreciate your family attending our wedding.'

She forced a smile to her lips, while her eyes scanned the interior of the cabin. Her father, his wife Mildred, her half-sister Julie, Julie's husband Tom and their son plus Mark's wife Mary and her three girls were all on board.

But the biggest surprise to Amber was Tim's presence. In a flurry of greetings and with the aircraft door closing and the captain announcing take-off, it was some time before Amber caught her breath long enough to look up at Lucas, who had somehow manoeuvred her into a seat and fastened her seat belt.

'Why didn't you tell me? I thought this was supposed to be a quick civil wedding and an even quicker divorce,' she hissed as the roar of the engines signalled lift-off. 'Why on earth involve my family?'

Lucas's dark head bent towards her, one arm resting lightly over her slender shoulders. 'I am Greek, we are very family orientated,' his deep voice murmured against her ear. 'And, though I have lost my family, it would be unthinkable to exclude yours,' he declared, the warmth of his breath against her face sending her pulse-rate rocketing.

Amber stared at him, and Lucas stared levelly back at her, his hooded black eyes giving nothing away.

'But Tim as well, I thought…' She didn't know what she thought.

'He is your lifelong friend,' he explained with a casual shrug of his broad shoulders. Against her will, Amber's eyes were drawn to those same shoulders, straining under the cotton knit polo shirt, and gulped. The popping of a champagne cork was a welcome diversion.

Seat belts were unfastened, and the luxurious comfort of the private jet was enjoyed by everyone. Amber found herself seated on a soft hide sofa, with Lucas apparently glued to her side. She could feel the heat of his thigh through the thin silk of her dress, and almost snapped the stewardess's hand off when she offered her a glass of champagne. Amber needed to cool down quick…

The flight took on a party mood, champagne flowed freely, and toasts were drunk to the engaged couple. Lucas responded by taking the opportunity to sweep Amber into his arms and kiss her thoroughly, much to the delight of everyone except Amber. Who, as soon as she could without it looking obvious, got to her feet and put some distance between them. She engaged Mary in conversation only to have the woman gush all over her, because her three girls were to be bridesmaids.

It was the first Amber had heard of it, and she downed another glass of champagne as more toasts were drunk to just about everyone.

When Sir David raised his glass and offered a toast to his son Mark who unfortunately could not be with them, Amber glanced warily across the cabin to where Lucas was in conversation with Tim. Her fiancé lifted his head, his black eyes clashing with hers as he raised his glass to her, and smiled a chilling smile that was more of a warning.

But, fortified with another couple of glasses of champagne and a delightful cold lunch to settle her nervous stomach, Amber had forgotten the moment by the time the aircraft landed.

'Are you all right?' Lucas asked softly, his hand on her elbow as he guided her towards one of the waiting cars.

'Yes, never better.' Amber flashed him a smile—somewhere over Europe she had given up worrying, or some time after the fourth glass of champagne. 'Where are we going or is that another surprise?' she asked blithely.

Handing her into the back seat of a luxurious chauffeur-driven, air-conditioned car, Lucas lowered his long length in beside her, and, casually throwing his arm over her shoulders, he hauled her into his side. 'We are going to the latest Karadines luxury hotel complex, about an hour's drive up the coast from Athens.' He looked down into her flushed, beautiful face and his eyes gleamed with triumph, and something else Amber was too inebriated to recognise.

'Does that suit you?' he asked with an indulgent smile.

Lucas Karadines could afford to be indulgent. He congratulated himself as he settled her pliant body more comfortably against him; his long fingers lightly squeezed her upper arm. He had her. Amber was here in his car, in his country, and tomorrow she would be his in every way known to man. 'Amber?' he queried, but her eyes had closed and she was fast asleep.

Amber's eyelids flickered half open and closed again. She nuzzled her head into the warm human pillow, blissfully aware of Lucas's arms enfolding her in a warm embrace.

She opened her eyes again, and let her lips brush against the strong brown column of his throat. Her tongue flicked

out, and tasted the warm, smooth skin. Amber breathed in
the familiar masculine scent of him and sighed with pleasure. She felt the tightening of his fingers at her waist and
stirred, tilting her head back to look up into his much-
loved face. 'Lucas,' she murmured his name, still in that
no man's land between sleep and wakefulness.

Through half-closed eyes, she saw his dark head de-
scending, the mobile mouth with just the hint of a smile,
and her tongue stroked out over her softly parted lips in
sensual anticipation.

His mouth covered hers, and she sighed her acceptance
as his tongue gently explored the soft dark interior, and
she reciprocated. His lips were firm yet sensuous, his touch
so light, she mused languidly. His strong hand closed over
her breast, and she groaned, the nipple peaking in instant
reaction to his touch. She snuggled closer and let her own
hand drop to his thigh and gently stroke upwards. She
heard his hiss of breath and felt his instant reaction. His
long, hard body was savagely tense; her slender fingers
traced the outline of his rampant arousal through the fabric
of his trousers. His dark head bent and he muttered something violent in Greek and captured her mouth again with
a raw passion, a ferocious urgency that took her by surprise. Her head swam and she could hardly breathe. Fire
scorched through her veins. She heard him moan, and the
blast of heat was overpowering. With a violent curse
Lucas lifted his head. Amber surfaced abruptly from a
whirlpool of passion.

A blast of hot air *had* invaded the air-conditioned interior of the car. The door was open...

'Come on, you two, we are waiting.' A deep masculine
voice laced with laughter echoed in Amber's head, and
suddenly she was wide awake. Appalled at what she was
doing, she jerked back and clasped her hands tightly to-

gether across her chest, staring into Lucas's dark face with horrified golden eyes.

'*Christo!* Don't move,' Lucas growled, his arms tightening around her, shielding his body with hers. 'Give me a moment,' he husked with one strong hand stroking slowly up and down her back, his breathing ragged. 'You have the most damnable timing, Amber,' he informed her, slowly withdrawing his arms from around her trembling body.

A rueful smile twisted his firm lips, but the heat in his hungry gaze as he stared into her upturned face was sent wild colour surging over her cheeks. Lucas still wanted her every bit as much as she wanted him. The realisation sent her into renewed shock.

'I must have been drunk,' she muttered, sliding back along the seat to her own side of the car, mortified that she had betrayed herself so publicly. For a moment she had travelled back in time to the younger Amber when she'd fallen madly in love for the first time and had believed her feelings were reciprocated. Hastily she lifted her hands and swept back the wild tumble of her hair behind her ears.

'Then I will have to make sure I feed you champagne for the rest of our lives.' Lucas drove raking fingers through his thick black hair, much the same as she had just done, and stared at her. Dark eyes met her bemused gold, his lips curved back over brilliant white teeth in a dazzling genuine smile, the like of which Amber had not seen in years, and her own eyes widened in wonder. 'But if you keep looking at me like that I think the champagne may be superfluous,' Lucas prompted softly. 'Come on.'

It was a very subdued Amber that stepped out of the car. How had she imagined for a second that she could marry Lucas and not go to bed with him, when a simple smile had her panting? Her knees felt weak and she was actually grateful when Lucas slid a strong arm around her waist as he introduced her to the man who had so casually interrupted them.

'This is Joe, my right-hand man, and tomorrow my best man.'

Amber looked up into the laughing grey eyes of the tall, brown-haired man. 'How do you do?' she said formally.

'Great for having finally met you,' he responded with a trace of an American accent.

'You're American,' Amber said stiltedly. If she had not been feeling so embarrassed she would have immediately liked the man.

'Greek-American and you are very English, and very beautiful, exactly as Lucas described you.' He smiled broadly. 'Pity he saw you first.'

'Cut that out, Joe; the lady is mine,' Lucas said possessively. Amber watched as the two men exchanged an expressive look, and then they were all entering the vast foyer of the hotel.

Immediately Amber's family surrounded them, while Joe, with a few swift commands, had their luggage taken care of. Lucas confidently listed the features of the complex at Sir David's request. Set in two hundred acres with its own golf course, shooting range, and private beach with every kind of water sport available, it was a holiday paradise. Private chalets were scattered all around the complex. But he had arranged for everyone to stay in a number of suites in the main hotel building, as it was more convenient.

Without a word Lucas took hold of Amber's arm and led her towards a lift. The doors swung open as if waiting for his arrival and he urged her inside.

For the sake of something to say, Amber offered, 'Joe seems a really nice man.'

The look Lucas cast her held a hint of wry acceptance and something more she did not recognise. 'Implying I am not?' he taunted gently.

'I never said that.' She tensed, suddenly feeling claustrophobic in the small enclosed lift.

'Relax, Amber—I was joking. All the ladies like Joe. The trouble is, he likes all the ladies. *All* being the operative word.' Lucas, his eyes glinting, flicked Amber a teasing glance, asking her to share his humour.

Lucas in a light-hearted mood was impossible to resist, and a reluctant smile parted her full lips. She could imagine Joe as a ladies' man with no trouble. He had the good looks and easygoing charm, and the banter girls the world over fell for.

'And of course you don't,' she mocked.

His hand reached out and caught hold of Amber's, spreading her fingers as he threaded his own through hers. 'No, I only want one.' And the look he cast down was serious, his black eyes penetrating on her lovely face. 'And I've got you,' he murmured, leading her out of the lift. Amber was powerless to control the sudden acceleration in her pulse, or to deny his hand holding hers was oddly reassuring.

Twenty minutes later she stood in the centre of the elegantly furnished sitting room, and looked around in wide-eyed awe. 'It's magnificent, Lucas.' She turned her beautiful face towards him and grinned. 'It's bigger than my cottage. I could live in here.' He had just given her a tour of the suite. From the long balcony with magnificent views over the bay, through the stylish bedroom with a king-sized bed, from which she had hastily dashed out into the bathroom, with double shower and whirlpool bath all in the finest marble.

'I'm glad you like it. My only regret is I cannot stop and share it with you now. But have patience, tomorrow will be a different story,' he declared with all the arrogance of a supremely confident man. 'And the experience will be all the more erotic for the anticipation, I promise.'

Amber flinched. After her performance in the car it was hardly surprising; he thought she was a pushover. But then Lucas was a typical alpha male, strikingly handsome, lethally sexy, wealthy, sophisticated, and great in bed, and the combination was irresistible. She doubted he'd ever met a woman in his life that would not be happy to fall into his arms at the first opportunity. But it galled her to think he thought she was one, and that he had to apologise for leaving!

She straightened her shoulders, her proud gaze narrowing on his face. 'Providing I am still here. After all, there is nothing to stop me changing my mind, a woman's prerogative and all that,' Amber pointed out. That should give the arrogant devil something to worry about.

Tall and powerful even in casual clothes, Lucas watched her, not a flicker of any emotion showing on his handsome, hard-boned face. 'I'm sure you can leave,' he said softly, moving swiftly across to where she stood. 'But you won't.' Tilting her chin with one long finger, he added, 'That is the second reason for your family's attendance at the ceremony. You might want to walk out on me, but no way will you walk out on them…' He shook his dark head. 'Leaving them dependent on my hospitality. I know you too well, Amber.'

Amber squirmed at her own stupidity. She had actually bought his fairy story on the plane about her family. His second reason was much more believable. The devious devil—in that second she hated him. 'You really are a swine,' she hissed. The fact that his assumption was also correct did nothing for her temper.

His perfectly chiselled features froze into impassivity, but not before she saw the flare of anger in the depths of the hard black eyes that held hers.

'It won't work.' Lucas's fingers tightened slightly on her chin. 'I told you earlier, I am not going to argue with you, so stop trying.' His thumb traced along her full lower lip, and she could not repress the shiver that rippled through her.

'You want me and I want you, so stop fighting it. With our history it is inevitable.'

'No,' she denied, but her body inexplicably swayed forward like a moth to a flame, her golden gaze captured by the simmering sensuality in his night-black eyes.

'Yes.' Lucas smiled a wry sexy twist to his firm lips. His hand dropped from her face. He ached for her with a hunger, a pain she had no knowledge of. But he dared not touch her again. Not yet! He'd made one mistake, and he was not about to risk making another until he had his ring safely on her finger. 'But not now—I have some business to attend to in Athens, but I will be back to take you to dinner at nine. If you need anything, speak to Joe or Reception.' Lucas bent and dropped a swift kiss on her full lips and left.

Tense and frustrated at her own inability to resist him, Amber paced the length of the room and back, her mind a seething mass of conflicting emotions. Was she a woman or a wimp? A few hours ago she'd been determined her marriage to Lucas would be in name only. But one touch and she melted like ice in a desert. And he, damn him, knew it!

By eight in the evening Amber was almost at boiling-point. The first shock had been Reception delivering a wedding dress to her room and a handful of bridesmaid dresses, closely followed by Julie and Mary and her daughters. Amber had stood in the middle of the room like a statue as the other two women had shoved the girls into masses of white froth while Julie had explained it had all been Lucas's idea. He was such a considerate man, she had rhapsodised.

Apparently, he had explained, because it was a second marriage for him Amber was being stubborn and insisting on keeping it low-key—a simple suit had been mentioned. But he did not want to deprive Amber of a white wedding. So he'd asked Julie to choose the gowns for the occasion.

Any thought of depriving the young girls of being bridesmaids or of doing a bunk on Amber's part had been quickly dispelled by the constant visitors to her room: her father, Mildred, everyone, and all in favour of the wedding.

Amber lay in the decadent marble bath, and steamed her temper as hot as the water. Finally she stepped out and, picking up a large fluffy towel, wrapped it around her naked body, and then, using the hair-dryer provided, she spent the next ten minutes drying her long hair. Walking back into the bedroom, she picked white lace briefs from the drawer and stepped into them. She didn't have much time and she wanted to be ready before Lucas arrived. Amber did not want him in her room again; once was enough for one day.

Quickly she withdrew from the wardrobe a blue silk jersey halter-necked dress, and slipped it over her head. Turning, she glanced at her reflection in the wall mirror, smoothing the clinging fabric down over her slender hips. The skirt ended a few inches above her knee, and she adjusted the bodice over her firm breasts, eyeing the cleavage with a wry look. Either she was getting fatter or the dress had shrunk in the wash. With a toss of her head, she dismissed her worries and slipped her feet into matching blue open-toed sandals.

It took only minutes to apply moisturiser to her smooth skin, a touch of mascara to her long lashes, and a plain pink lipgloss completed her make-up. With the ease of long habit, she brushed her long hair back behind her ears and let it fall loose down her back. She fastened the gold Rolex watch, a present from her father, around her wrist. Five to nine, she made it, and, walking into the sitting room, she picked up her purse and left.

Luck was with her, a lift was waiting. Amber walked in and pressed the down button and seconds later she stepped out into the foyer. Julie and her husband and the whole crowd immediately surrounded her. Joe appeared and, heading straight for Amber, he took her arm. 'You look sensational. Where's Lucas?'

'I don't know,' she told the truth. Then she did know, when a strong arm curved around her waist.

'I'm here, Joe, you can unhand the lady now. I've got her.'

Amber tensed, her heart missing a beat. Slowly she turned her head. 'Lucas,' she greeted him.

'Amber, darling, you couldn't wait, you had to come down to meet me—how sweet.' The devilish light in his dark eyes should have warned her. He curved her close into his hard body, crushing her up against him as his dark head swooped and his lips claimed hers.

Amber's pulse went from normal to the speed of light, and then he lifted his head; though he still held her hard against him and she could not help but be aware of his instant, shameless arousal. 'You're sex mad,' she muttered angrily. 'And you had no right to get Julie to buy a wedding dress.'

He silenced her by claiming her mouth again in a long passionate kiss, and when he finally let her up for air she was boneless. It didn't matter how often he touched her, it was always the same. There had always been a devastating chemical reaction between them, and that had not changed in the intervening years. 'What do you think you are doing?' she croaked.

'Not what I want to be doing, that's for sure,' Lucas said bluntly in her ear, and then very slowly eased her away from him.

Her face scarlet, Amber wanted the ground to open and swallow her up. How dared he embarrass her like that in front of her family? Eyes flashing angrily, she looked at Lucas and caught her breath. In a superbly tailored white dinner jacket and narrow black trousers that clung to his thighs and accentuated the long length of his legs, he looked magnificent. A perfect example of a man—the slight dilation of his pupils still evident, although he had controlled his body, only added to his aura of predatory masculine power.

'You look ravishing, Amber.' His dark eyes raked her from head to toe. 'I am a very lucky man.' Lucas smiled— for the audience, Amber thought, but said nothing as he caught her hand and tucked it under his arm.

Dinner was probably superb, Amber decided almost two hours later. It was a pity she had no idea what she'd eaten. The *maître d'* had arranged for a long rectangular table to be set at one end of the elegant dining room so the whole party could eat together. Seated at Lucas's side at the top of the table, she had smiled and chatted and prayed for the evening to end.

'You must try this, *agape mou*.' Lucas's husky drawl

had all the women at the table swooning, while Amber felt like a cat on a hot tin roof. If he put his finger in her mouth one more time she swore she would bite it off.

Finally, when the meal was over and he called her his love for the umpteenth time, and let his long fingers stray over her breast supposedly to smooth back a strand of her hair, Amber turned in her seat and raised her golden eyes to his. 'You are so good to me, Lucas,' she said, and delivered a hard kick to his shin under the table.

Lucas threw back his head and laughed out loud. 'Really, Amber, you are priceless!'

She wasn't priceless, she was furious and frustrated and tingling all over in a semi-permanent state of arousal, because of his tricks.

'Hey, cut us in—what's the joke?' Joe asked with a grin.

'Private, strictly private,' Lucas responded, and settled gleaming dark eyes on Amber. 'It is only between my fiancée and I. Isn't that right, Amber?'

To everyone else it was a casual comment, but to Amber, with his intent gaze lingering on her face, it was very definitely a warning. Their war was private and nothing must upset the success of the evening. She picked up her wineglass and drained it, avoiding his eyes.

'By the way, Lucas, you will have to leave before midnight,' Sir David remarked as they were all being served with coffee after the meal. 'Traditionally it is unlucky to see the bride before the ceremony on the day of the wedding.'

'Well, I am all for tradition, so at midnight I'll make my way back to my lonely bed,' Lucas drawled with mock sorrow, and everyone laughed, except Amber who could only manage a stiff smile.

The urge to smash through the smooth façade he

showed to their guests raged through her. How could they not see the deception behind the clever, striking face? The feeling of being trapped was almost overpowering and she sighed with relief when a trio of musicians arrived and took up positions on the small stage set at the back of the small square dance-floor at one end of the elegant dining room and started to play. Chairs were pushed back, and to Amber's delight Tim appeared at her side.

'Dance with me, Amber. We have hardly had a chance to talk,' Tim asked. With a brief glance at Lucas, he added, 'If you don't mind.'

'Of course he doesn't mind,' Amber answered for Lucas, leaping to her feet. To escape Lucas's overpowering presence for a few moments was just what she needed. Grasping Tim's hand, she almost dragged him onto the dance-floor.

The lights had been dimmed and quite a few people were dancing. Amber slipped into Tim's arms, and felt as if she were home. 'Thank God!' she sighed, and, looking up into his familiar face and sparkling blue eyes, she smiled her first genuine smile of the evening. 'It's great to see you; I had no idea you were coming.'

'Lucas called me last week and told me your good news. My favourite girl getting married! How could I refuse? Then again, your fiancé is a very persuasive man, I doubt anyone dares refuse him.'

'You've got that right,' Amber said with feeling, her smile vanishing.

'Hardly the response I would have expected from a woman in love,' Tim stated quietly, and, tightening his arms around her waist as they moved slowly to the music, he asked, 'What's wrong, Amber?'

'Nothing,' she murmured. It wasn't fair to involve Tim in her problems.

'Come on, it's me, your best pal. I know you better than you know yourself. I've watched you all night—your laughter was forced and your smile strained. That is not like you at all. You're the most genuine person I know.'

Moisture glazed her eyes. 'Thanks for that, Tim.' And suddenly she had the overwhelming need to confess everything. 'You're right, Tim.' And as they moved around the dance-floor she told him about Spiro's will and the consequences of it.

'That's Spiro for you,' Tim remarked dryly. 'Even in death he causes mayhem. But that is not your problem, Amber. All you need to ask yourself is, do you love Lucas? Everything else is superfluous; believe me, I know.'

'Yes, I never stopped loving him,' Amber admitted huskily, the sadness in her voice unmistakable. 'But Lucas had never loved me. I thought he did, and you know what happened. He fell in love with someone else.'

'I'm not so sure about that,' Tim contradicted. 'Lucas Karadines is a very traditional Greek male, and at the time he would have done anything to humour his father—the man was dying. He went to great lengths to hide Spiro's sexuality from the old man. Marrying the girl his father approved of would seem a likely thing for Lucas to do. As for loving her, he might have thought he did, but we men are just as likely as women to mistake our true feelings.'

'Since when did you become such an expert on the sexes?' Amber asked dryly.

'Since I made a huge mistake with Spiro that could have cost me my life.'

'But you did truly love him,' Amber responded. 'I was there, remember.'

'No, it was friendship and infatuation, and the only reason I stayed so long was because Spiro, as the dominant partner, kept telling me we were in love. But once in New York and watching how he behaved, I discovered I didn't actually care enough to even be jealous, and I realised it wasn't real love I felt for him. I know the difference now. I have a new partner, David.' His blue eyes lit up with happiness as he continued. 'He has a picture-framing business in Newcastle and what we share is true love. So you see, Amber, we can all make quite horrendous mistakes.'

Amber looked up into his lovable face, believing him. 'I am glad for you, but it doesn't really help me. Lucas loved his wife—he can't even bring himself to talk about her death.'

'But she is dead, Amber, and she can't come between you any more. Lucas wants a flesh-and-blood woman.' He held her slightly away from him, his blue eyes roaming the luscious length of her, camping it up with mocking male appreciation. 'And you are certainly that!'

Amber grinned at his teasing; she could not help it.

'Look at him—he is watching me like a hawk.' Tim gestured with his head, and, glancing across the room, Amber saw Lucas rising up from the table, his whole attention fixed on her. 'Believe me, Amber, he wants you and badly. He and I had a long talk last week. I'm sure he loves you even if he does not want to admit it. Take a chance.'

'Take a chance on what?' Lucas's deep, melodious voice broke into the conversation. 'You are already taking a big chance, Tim, dancing with my fiancée for so long. If you don't mind.'

'My pleasure.' Tim grinned and, leaning forward, he dropped a swift kiss on Amber's nose. 'Go for it,' he whispered before placing her hand in Lucas's.

'Are you sure that guy is gay? I saw the way he looked

at you,' Lucas queried, slipping a long arm around her waist, and clasping her other hand in his, holding her close to his strong body.

Tilting her head back, she looked up into his oddly serious face. 'Jealous of Tim?' she prompted with a chuckle.

'I'm no fool; if your closest male friend had been straight I would never have invited him in a million years,' he declared bluntly.

Amber couldn't help it, she burst out laughing.

'I'm glad I amuse you,' Lucas said simply. 'I have been trying to all night.'

The hint of a smile quirked the corners of his mobile mouth as his hand laced with hers and raised it to his lips. He brushed a kiss along her knuckles, before moving her effortlessly to the soft strains of the music.

'Is that what you were doing?' Seducing her more likely, Amber thought, and slid a slender arm up around his neck, tangling her fingers in the silky black hair at his nape. 'I would have called it *teasing*.' She pouted and did some teasing of her own, relaxing against him, and moving her hips in an exaggerated sway to the rhythm of the music. Her golden eyes gleamed mischievously up at Lucas.

His black eyes glittered over her lovely face. 'Amber.' One hand caressed her back down her spine, curving her in closer to the hard strength of his body, and heat pooled in her belly. 'Watch it! You're playing a dangerous game,' his husky voice drawled as he curled their joined fists against her breast.

Her sensitive flesh swelled and her nipples peaked into tight buds against the smooth fabric of her gown as desire, sharp and physical, scorched between them. Amber could not drag her eyes away from his. She wanted him so much, she trembled. 'I don't play games,' she whispered, and then, with courage she had not known she possessed, she asked, 'but what about you?' He'd played with her emotions once before; she had no reason to suppose it would be any different this time.

CHAPTER NINE

LUCAS had hurt Amber so much before, it terrified her as she waited for his answer. But Tim had told her to take a chance; after all, Christina was dead and Lucas was very much alive.

Something she was made vividly aware of the next second as, dropping her hand, he placed his through the silken fall of her hair to curve around the nape of her neck and tip her head back. 'No, I never play games,' he contradicted fiercely while his other hand, low on the base of her spine, urged her hard against him. 'Does this feel like a game?' His lean hips moved urgently against her, making her aware of his arousal. 'Do you think I willingly walk around in this state aching for you? The chemistry between us is as strong as it always was, always will be.'

'Not always.' The memory of him walking out on her was ever present.

Lucas stilled, giving up any pretence of dancing. 'Yes, even then,' he confessed harshly. He knew exactly what she meant, and he was ashamed of his behaviour, but at the time he had been too blindly arrogant to see the truth. He had decided it was time he fell in love and married, and had set about doing it exactly the same way as he pursued a business deal. He had been so confident he'd been doing the right thing. Pleasing his father, and expecting it to please himself.

'No,' Amber denied. 'Don't bother lying.' It was all a game to Lucas, anything to get his own way. 'I was *there*, remember,' she prompted scathingly. 'You said I was dis-

139

gusting, a hedonist. You as good as called me a whore,' she fumed, all the old anger and resentment bubbling to the surface.

Lucas's arm around her waist jerked tighter. His superb bone structure tautened and something that looked almost like pain glinted in his night-black eyes. 'I was disgusted with *myself*, Amber, never you. Spiro's statement after my engagement party that he was going to marry you had enraged me, but deep down I suspected it was a lie. Though it did not stop me using it as an excuse to see you again. I had to make sure, I told myself, and, seeing you so strong and defiant and desirable, I was lost to all reason, consumed by such an irresistible passion that nothing else mattered. I betrayed my fiancée, and I hated myself, so I took it out on you. You have to believe me, and if I hurt you with my brutally callous remarks I am truly sorry.'

If... He'd almost destroyed her, and he had not even realised he'd been doing it...and yet, looking up into his taut, sombre face, she believed him. Plus he had actually done it, actually managed to say *I'm sorry*. For once the arrogant, all-powerful Lucas Karadines was admitting he was as susceptible to making a mistake as any ordinary mortal was.

'Amber, I swear it was never my intention to hurt you, then or now. We are getting married tomorrow.' His sensual mouth twisted wryly. 'Can we at least try to forget the past and make it work? Make it real.'

His strong hand moved restlessly up and down her spine and with the heat, the strength of him enveloping her, she was tempted to agree.

'Please,' Lucas pleaded for the first time in his life. He had behaved like the worst kind of hide-bound, chauvinistic fool when he had let this woman go. Equating great sex with a girlfriend, but talking himself into loving what he had considered an acceptable wife. Now he knew better: love was an illusion; lust was reality. He might not like the way Amber affected him so instantly. But he was not fool enough to believe he could live with her without making love to her. He was no masochist.

Amber saw his eyes darken. She knew what he wanted, what he was asking, and was dizzied by the sensations snaking through her. She placed a hand on his shirt-front to steady herself. Involuntarily her hand stroked up over the front of his chest, feeling the uneven pounding of his heart beneath the fine silk of his shirt. He wanted her, and in all honesty Amber knew she ached for him. She was older now and she no longer saw Lucas as the perfect, infallible, godlike male she had years ago, yet she still loved him.

She was under no illusion as to why he was marrying her. He was not prepared to trust Amber's word she would sell Spiro's shares to him. It was ingrained in his character to trust no one; an asset in the top echelons of the business world, but on a personal level more of a liability, though Lucas would never see it as such. But the real question was, was she mature enough to forget all her old bitterness and anger, and take what was on offer? A few months of sexual pleasure at least, and maybe, just maybe Lucas might come to love her. Dared she take the chance?

'Amber...' his long fingers tangled in the silky gold locks of her hair, he urged her face to his '...what do you say?'

She could say no! And deprive herself of six months of pleasure and probably the only sex she would get in her life. She looked into his eyes, and was fascinated by the tinge of vulnerability that even the sensual hunger blazing in their depths could not hide. Or she could say yes! And pray she was mature enough to walk away with her pride intact when the time came.

Her golden gaze meshed with his. 'Yes, I suppose...'

Whatever else she might have said was lost as Lucas covered her mouth with his own, his tongue prising her lips apart, thrusting and tasting with a simmering sensuality, again and again.

'This is becoming a habit,' a laughing Joe exclaimed. 'Break it up, you two, it is late.'

Lucas groaned, and lifted his head. He eased his hand from Amber's nape but still kept his arm around her waist. 'We appear to be the floor show, sweetheart,' he husked, brushing the long fall of her chestnut hair carefully back off her face.

'Oh, heavens!' Blushing bright red, Amber tried to ease away, horribly aware the music was no longer playing, and everyone was watching them with varying degrees of amusement.

Lucas grinned and, clasping her around the waist with both hands, he stepped back, his dark eyes, blazing with masculine triumph, flicking over her. 'It's all right, you look decent,' he murmured huskily. 'But Joe is right. It is late, and I have to leave you before the witching hour, according to your father. If I want to be lucky, and I *am* going to be lucky tomorrow night...' He arched one ebony brow wickedly.

Amber's blush could have lit the room. She walked back to the table with Lucas on legs that shook. Any thought of trying to pretend she was immune to him was banished for ever from her brain.

'Well, any lingering doubts I had about the haste of this wedding are well and truly put to rest, old man.' Sir David slapped Lucas on the back. 'But in future I would try to be a little more circumspect, if I were you.' He chuckled.

'I will, Sir,' Lucas agreed and the two men exchanged a very masculine smug grin. 'And look after Amber for me until tomorrow.' Bending his dark head, he pressed a swift kiss on her brow. 'Go to bed. It's late.'

She did not need looking after, nor did she need to be told to go to bed. But, then again, after the exhibition she had just made of herself, maybe she did.

Noon the next day Amber stood in front of the dressing mirror, and barely recognised herself. The sides of her long hair had been swept up into an intricate crown of curls threaded through with perfect white rosebuds and tiny satin ribbons, and the rest left to fall in gentle curls down her back. Her make-up was light but perfect. The wedding dress was a dream, the soft fabric draped narrowly across her shoulders, exposing just a hint of the creamy mounds of her breasts. Cut on the bias, it shimmied across the shapely length of her body to end at her ankles in a scalloped border embroidered in a rose pattern. She glanced around the havoc of the room, and smiled at the three young bridesmaids. They were standing in a stiff line, terrified of spoiling their finery; their dresses flounced like crinolines from fitted waists and copied the embroidery of the bridal gown.

Someone handed Amber a posy of ivory roses mixed with baby's breath and her father appeared at her side, resplendent in a pale grey suit.

'You look beautiful, Amber. I am so proud to be your father and I want you to know—I deeply regret all the wasted years when I was not there for you. Especially now when I am losing you again.' Tears glazed her golden eyes, and she sniffed as he took her hand and tugged it under his arm, adding, 'Time to go, Amber.'

Suddenly the enormity of what she was about to do hit her and for a second she panicked. 'But I don't even know where I am going,' Amber wailed.

Hoots of laughter greeted her comment and someone shouted, 'Joe has it all arranged,' as everyone moved towards the door.

Amber gasped—it was like something out of a Hollywood movie. Joe had done a superb job. A secluded corner of the vast gardens of the hotel was set out with chairs for the guests, the centre aisle leading to a raised dais covered with a delicate arched pergola beautifully decorated with hundreds of tiny white roses and vines.

The three little girls were solemnly walking down the aisle sprinkling rose petals from decorated baskets, and then it was Amber's turn.

Straightening her shoulders, Amber took a tighter grasp of her father's arm and stepped forward, her gaze fixed on the tall black-haired man standing with his back to her in front of the celebrant. Then he turned to watch her approach.

The clear blue sky and the blinding sun added to Amber's feeling of unreality and only hazily was she aware of the guests seated either side of the aisle, her glance captured by Lucas's intent, unwavering gaze. He was magnificent in an immaculate pale grey silk suit, and white shirt, and a grey silk tie shot through with blue. His thick black hair had been neatly trimmed and he looked exactly what he was: a mature, sophisticated Greek businessman, while Amber, on the other hand, was shaking like a jelly with nerves.

It was stupid, she knew. She'd lived with the man for a year, for heaven's sake! She should not be intimidated by what was really a simple civil ceremony—it was not as if she were marrying him for life.

But as her father left her at Lucas's side, Amber knew that for her it would be a life sentence. She would never love any man the way she loved Lucas. Looking up into his darkly handsome face, she had to blink hard to stop emotional tears blinding her eyes. 'You've had your hair cut.' She said the first thing that came into her head to cover her emotions.

His black eyes widened in surprise and then his lips parted over brilliant white teeth in a beaming smile. 'I'm so glad you noticed,' he murmured for her ears only. 'I was afraid you might have changed your mind, and not deign to look at me.'

Lucas afraid was a novel notion, but she did not have time to dwell on it as she listened to the celebrant and surprisingly a priest appeared. Amber was too nervous to take much in but she must have made the right response. Lucas took hold of her hand and slipped a gold band on her ring finger, and indicated she should return the favour by placing a ring on his finger. Surprised he would want to wear a ring, she glanced up and was captivated by the blaze of emotion in his dark eyes. She hesitated for a moment and Lucas covered her hand with his free one and helped her slip the ring on his finger.

'My wife at last,' he murmured. Then gathered her into his arms and kissed her. It was a kiss like no other, firm but tender, sensual and seeking. Amber's head swam, her pulse raced, her full lips parting to welcome him.

'Break it up, you two. You still have plenty of time for that later. We have to party.'

To Amber's chagrin, once again it was Joe who'd brought them back to their senses. Flushing scarlet, she glanced wildly around at all the grinning faces, then tilted her head to look up at Lucas.

'You really are a blushing bride now,' Lucas said wryly. 'My fault—I got carried away.' Her heart gave a curious lurch at seeing the glittering intensity of his gaze, igniting sparks of sensual awareness through her whole body. 'But you are the most beautiful bride. I don't have the words to tell you how much it means to me you are mine.' His voice was thickened with emotion and he lifted her hand to his mouth and kissed the wedding band.

Amber wanted to believe his sentiment was genuine but, tearing her eyes from his, she mumbled, 'Yes, well, thank you.' She loved him but trusting him again was something else...

The speeches were over, and the wedding reception had taken on the air of a joyous feast. Lucas led Amber from one table to another to say their goodbyes. Amber was stunned at the number of people. Lucas appeared to have a remarkable number of friends, all Greek, and as she could not speak the language she simply nodded and smiled.

It was a relief when Lucas curved his large hands possessively around her shoulders and murmured, 'It's time you changed, we have to leave in a few minutes.'

'Leave. What for?' Amber queried. She glanced up and saw the amusement gleaming in his black eyes, and she simply stared rather helplessly back at him.

Lucas chuckled. 'Because the honeymoon is the best part of the wedding, my sweet.'

Julie burst out laughing. 'Come on, Amber, I'll help you change.' Before Amber knew it she was back in the bedroom of the suite.

Amber removed her bridal gown, and with Julie's help managed to remove the rosebuds from her hair. Five minutes later her hair was brushed, but a little on the wild side because of the curls. Julie was holding an elegant cream trouser suit up for her inspection.

'A present from your husband. Put it on.'

A silk and linen mix—the designer label told Amber it was incredibly expensive. The tiny silk camisole that left her midriff bare prevented her from wearing a bra, but with the jacked fastened it looked great. Chic casual and Amber wondered again where they were going. Two hours later she knew…

'So. What do you think? ' Lucas demanded, his black eyes alight with pleasure. 'Isn't she beautiful? I only bought her a few months ago, and I have not really had the time to try her out.' The pride and admiration in his voice were unmistakable.

Amber stood on the wooden deck and looked around. They had driven to a marina along the coast, and Lucas had just finished showing her around his latest toy—a thirty-foot motor cruiser.

'The joy of this is…' Lucas continued, his handsome face animated '…it does not need a crew, I can handle it myself, and the two of us will have no problem. Everyone sails around the islands, but I thought we could explore the mainland coastline, stopping off to see the places of interest, of course. It will be fun.'

He was wearing cream cotton trousers and a short-sleeved blue checked shirt. His legs were planted slightly apart on the deck. He looked so sexy, the sheer size and virile strength of him hit her like a punch in the stomach. Amber hadn't the heart to tell him she'd never been to sea before, other than on a ferry. For all she knew, she might get seasick.

'It sounds very nice, but I don't know much about boats,' she managed to say, suddenly realising just what kind of intimacy she was inviting if she agreed. She had seen the galley was small and compact, the saloon was beautifully furnished, and comfortable, but not huge. There was one large cabin with a very big bed, a shower and toilet. One small cabin with a couple of bunks and a lot of computer equipment.

'You don't need to.' Lucas caught both of her hands and cradled them in his own. 'I will teach you everything; you will love it, I promise.'

Standing barefoot on the deck, Lucas had insisted she remove her shoes, declaring they were unsuitable for the wood deck, and, with the warmth of his hands enfolding hers, she felt totally out of her depth in more ways than one. 'Yes, well...'

Lucas drew her into his arms, pulling her close so the top of her head tucked under his chin. 'Great. I had intended taking you to a very exclusive holiday island in the Bahamas, but yesterday when I saw your suitcase and you said you only needed a few clothes because you intended to bum around and do nothing, I thought of this.'

'I missed out on the Bahamas!' Amber exclaimed, flashing a mock protesting glance up at him, only to chuckle when she saw his teasing expression.

'I will take you another time,' Lucas countered, his dark eyes suddenly serious. 'I am going to do everything in my power to make sure you never miss out on anything life has to offer ever again.' He gathered her in even closer, and Amber was utterly transfixed by the burning desire in his eyes. A desire Lucas was doing nothing to hide.

She gasped, a soft sound, her lips parting as awareness shivered though her. Lucas lowered his mouth down to hers, and stole the breath from her body.

The kiss didn't last long, but when he drew away and said gruffly, 'Let's go below,' with a nod of her head Amber mutely agreed.

Lucas wanted her, and, dear God, she wanted him. She wanted to feel that sensuous mouth on her own again, those elegant hands on her naked flesh, feel once more the exquisite pleasure only Lucas could provide. There was no point in denying it.

He didn't give her time to change her mind. Clasping her hand, he led her quickly down into the living quarters. His steps were urgent as he hurried her through the salon and into the bedroom.

Kicking the door shut behind him, he let go of her hand and reached for her, quickly opening the buttons of her jacket, and he slid it down her shoulders to drop unnoticed on the floor.

Amber gasped, her breathing was fractured, her pulse was racing, her breasts swelling against the silk camisole. His smouldering eyes burned a path down her body, taking in the bare midriff; at the same time his fingers deftly dealt with the fastening of her trousers. His dark head bent towards her and her lips parted in anticipation of his kiss, but instead he moved lower, his mouth closing over the tip of her silk-encased breast, sucking on it, then biting and nibbling, and her spine arched on a fierce shock of sensual pleasure.

He dropped to his knees, taking her trousers and briefs with him while his mouth slid from her breast to lick down over her bare midriff, and circle her navel, and lower.

'No, Lucas,' she tried to protest at the ultimate intimacy, even as a low erotic moan escaped her. His head jerked up, his black eyes smouldered. Standing up, he whipped the camisole over her head, and tumbled her naked body backwards onto the bed.

Lucas looked down at her, his passionate gaze roaming over every inch of her body as he swiftly stripped naked. 'You're perfect,' he growled, falling down to join her on the bed.

'So are you,' Amber murmured throatily, the sight of his big tanned body, hugely aroused, sending shivers of pleasurable anticipation arching though her.

He leant over her, his mouth capturing hers in a savagely hungry kiss that she welcomed like a sex-starved slave, her tongue tangling with his, relishing the devouring need that had always been between them. His hand slid down over her breast and stomach, along her slender thigh, parting her long legs. He touched her, and she shuddered, her body responding with a wanton life all of its own. She grasped his broad shoulders, her slender hands tracing down his long back, feeling the satin-smooth skin burning beneath her fingertips. She wanted him, wanted him now with a fierce, primitive need.

He broke the kiss. They fought for breath, his dark eyes holding hers asking the question and he saw the answer in her luminous golden gaze. With a low growl he lowered his head and sucked one rigid nipple into his mouth. Her back arched off the bed, and she was lost in the fiery sensations flooding through her. She never heard her own little whimpering cries of pleasure, as with hands and mouth Lucas ravished every inch of her body.

'You want me.' Lucas shifted his weight between her thighs, his arms straining either side of her pulsing body.

She was lost to all reason, her eyes burning like molten gold clung to his. 'Yes, yes, yes,' she pleaded, and involuntarily she lifted her long legs and wrapped them around his lean waist. Lucas thrust into her in one strong stroke, and she cried out at the power of his possession. He was there, where she ached for him.

He filled her, and moved in her in a wild pagan rhythm. Her legs wrapped tighter around his thrusting body as she soared ever higher and higher. Her arms reached for him, pulling his head down close enough for her mouth to meet his. Her tongue sought to repeat the rhythm of their bodies.

Lucas threw back his head, his battle for restraint evident in the damp sheen on the taut bronzed features. He watched her eagerly, as he drove feverishly harder, his hands grasping her buttocks, holding her in a grip of steel as she reached the peak. Her keening cry rending the air as the incredible tension snapped, her tight, pulsing muscles convulsed inside her taking Lucas with her in a fierce dynamic surge of powerful release that shook his great body, totally out of control.

It was a frantic coupling and together they clung in the shuddering aftermath, until finally, their sweat-slicked bodies entwined, they both fought to breathe air into laboured lungs, the pounding of two hearts together.

Amber let her arms fall weakly to the bed as reality intruded. But it wasn't love and she had to remember that, and she tried to move.

Lucas rolled off her, and, lying down beside her, he gathered her tenderly into the curve of his body. She tried to ease away, but he hauled her closer. 'Lie still and let me hold you for a while,' he rasped in a throaty voice. 'My Amber, my sexy wife,' and the satisfaction in his tone was unmistakable.

'Wife,' Amber murmured, her golden eyes widening in surprise as she glanced up at him. The *sexy* she did not like at all—it reminded her too much of their past affair. But the *wife* she did like. Amber Karadines had a nice ring to it.

'Why the surprise?' Lucas grinned and, leaning over her, he kissed her very gently. 'We have just consummated our marriage, and that does make you my wife,' he drawled huskily. 'And if you give me a moment I will prove it to you all over again.' His eyes held hers, glinting with amusement, and Amber could not look away.

His suggestion of a repeat performance was enough to make her stomach curl and her breasts tingle, in shameful awareness of his promise of more sensual delights to come. 'I thought we were supposed to be going out to sea,' she reminded him, to take her mind off more erotic thoughts.

'I know,' he declared with a rueful grin. 'I'm beginning to wonder if a cruising holiday was such a great idea with only me to steer the boat.'

'Serves you right.' Amber laughed. 'You will be stuck at the wheel all day and night.'

'No way.' His head bent and he captured her mouth with his own.

Her lips parted, and her senses stirred again, a slow, deep, salacious curl of excitement that unfurled from her belly to ignite every nerve-end in her body. Lucas thought she was sex mad, always had. Why try to deny it? she wondered with stark reality—after all, this was what she wanted. She let her hands slide up over the bulging biceps to the wide shoulders and up to tangle in the thick black hair, and she held his head to hers and returned the kiss with equal fervour.

It was dark when Amber opened her eyes. She rolled over onto her stomach and discovered she was alone in the big bed. Then she realised the low noise she could hear was the sound of the engines, and the gentle motion of the boat told her he had put out to sea. Struggling to a sitting position, she surveyed the tangled mass of sheets, and her own slightly bruised naked body. She was just reaching for a sheet to cover her with when a light flicked on. Blinded by the light, she blinked for a moment.

'Good, you're awake. Come on.' Lucas smiled, walking over to the bed and lifting her bodily out of it.

'Wait a minute, what do you think you are doing?'

He lowered her down the length of his long body, and, with her feet on the not-so-firm floor, she glanced up at him. 'What time is it?'

'Time you started work, sailor. Hurry and get dressed

and meet me on the deck. If I stay here much longer—' his sparkling black eyes slid lasciviously over her naked body '—the boat will probably run aground.'

Ten days later, Amber leant on the rail of the boat with a cup of coffee in one hand, idly surveying the approaching shoreline. She had just showered and put on a fine lawn sarong skirt in blue and white with a blue bandeau around her breasts. Her long hair hung down her back in wet strands, because Lucas's precious boat with all mod cons did not possess a hair-dryer.

Stifling a big yawn, she lifted the cup to her mouth and took a sip. She grimaced as she swallowed. She needed the caffeine—an unrestricted diet of sex, sex and more sex could be pretty exhausting. For the first four days of their honeymoon, Lucas had anchored the boat in a secluded cove and they had lived on sex and the provisions on board. Lucas was almost insatiable, more so than she remembered, and, being brutally honest, she was no better herself.

He only had to look at her a certain way and they were straight into bed, or not necessarily the bed—the salon, the galley, the deck, a beach, even the sea, which she was surprised was possible. Maybe Lucas had been right about her all along—maybe she was a sex fiend, but then what did that make him?

She drained her coffee-cup and sighed. He certainly did not love her, the word hadn't been mentioned. Sometimes when she felt him deep inside her, possessing her, devouring her completely, she had to bite her tongue to stop crying out her love for him.

The tour of the Greek coastline had been a joke. The only sites Amber had seen were the sea and a naked Lucas. Her lips curled in a secretive smile—not that she was complaining. Lucas was fun to be with, and an experienced and inventive lover, and no woman could have dreamed of a more passionate honeymoon. And they had actually managed to travel through the Corinthian canal a couple of days ago.

They had stopped in the town of Corinth, and dined out for a change, and now they were heading for Karadines Island, and home.

Home was such an emotive word, and Amber felt longingly of her own little house in England. Amber was beginning to have severe doubts about lazing around all summer. It was all right for Lucas—he was going back to work after the weekend. He had told her last night. He had everything arranged: they would live on the island, and Lucas would travel into Athens most days by helicopter, but when he had to travel further afield Amber would go with him—at least until the children arrived, he'd laughed.

Amber had been stunned to think Lucas was actually considering her as the mother of his children. Or had he been joking...? She wasn't sure and so she'd mumbled something and changed the subject.

Before she'd left England she'd visited her doctor and started taking the pill, because, though loath to admit it, she'd known a platonic marriage was never going to work between them. And she wasn't fool enough to risk getting pregnant, much as she would love to have his child, until she was sure their relationship was going to last beyond the probate of Spiro's will. Lucas had let her down before, and she still didn't trust him...

Two large hands slid around her slender waist. 'Time to take up position.'

'What position would that be?' Amber queried teasingly as she turned in his arms to face him. He looked good enough to eat, showered and shaved and dressed in white

tailored shorts, and pale blue short-sleeved shirt, and his
sensuous mouth curved in a wicked smile.

'How about over the rail?' Lucas prompted, elevating
one dark brow enquiringly. 'I think that's one we have
missed.' His head dipped and he kissed her, and in an
exaggerated gesture bent her back over the rail.

'No, no,' she squealed with laughter as he nuzzled the
side of her neck. 'I was only joking.'

'I wasn't,' Lucas drawled mockingly, allowing her to
stand up.

'You're incorrigible.' Amber shook her head, but
grinned.

'I know. We will save the rail for later. In the meantime
would you go to the stern of the ship and be ready to
throw the line? We are going to dock in a few minutes.'

Only then did she notice they were a lot nearer the
shore. She could see the tiny harbour, and she was vividly
reminded of her other visit here with Tim and Spiro. It
seemed a lifetime ago now...

Twenty-two and in love for the first time, the only time.
Full of confidence and dressed up to the nines, she'd set
out to make Lucas Karadines notice her. Hoping and praying he would fall in love with her, and they would live
happily ever after. Then believing he had, she'd been bitterly disillusioned when their relationship had ended.

Who would have thought years later she would be coming back as Lucas's wife? Was she making the same mistake again? Amber wondered. No, because it wasn't the
same. She was no longer a young, trusting fool; she no
longer wore her heart on her sleeve. She and Lucas had a
mature adult relationship based mostly on sexual attraction
and a growing mutual respect. She kept her love and her
innermost thoughts to herself. Perhaps she had finally
grown up emotionally...

How times change, Amber mused sadly, her hazel eyes hazing with moisture. She was no longer the carefree girl who had first arrived on this island, but at least she was here. Poor Spiro was dead, and the woman Lucas had really loved, Christina, was also dead, both long before their time. Amber was the lucky one. She had a chance at a good marriage. It was up to her to take it. Life was too short for regrets.

CHAPTER TEN

'THROW it, Amber. Amber!' Lost in her thoughts, Amber had forgotten what she was supposed to be doing until an irate Lucas appeared at her side, grabbed the rope from her hand and threw it, muttering a string of curses in Greek.

She looked at him, and felt her breath catch in her throat. His hair was rumpled, his big muscled chest was bare and he looked supremely male and infinitely desirable.

'What were you thinking of?' Lucas whirled to face her. 'We almost hit the pier.'

'Sorry.' Amber smiled up at him, and, stepping forward, she looped her arms around his neck and, stretching up, placed a swift kiss on his firm lips. 'Guess,' she murmured teasingly.

His arms clasped her loosely around the waist, his dark eyes lit with laughter. 'I'd take you up on that, but the welcoming party awaits.'

Before she could respond, a heavy-set middle-aged man hurried along the deck to meet them carrying two garlands of wild flowers in his hands.

As he approached Lucas greeted him, and, taking Amber's hand, said, 'This is Tomso, he runs the bar-cum-store, and is in charge in my absence—a sort of mayor.'

Amber smiled as Tomso insisted on placing the garlands of flowers over their heads and leading them ashore. 'What did he say?' she asked Lucas as they stepped onto the old stone pier. The row of about a dozen or more whitewashed

157

houses lined one side of the earth road overlooking the bay were the same. But the twenty or so smiling faces of the locals waiting to greet them were a surprise.

'Every new Karadines bride arriving on the island has to be met with a garland of flowers; it's tradition.' Sliding an arm around her shoulders, and briefly kissing her smiling mouth, he added, 'We also have to walk to the villa.'

A great cheer went up as Lucas led her along the road, and suddenly Amber wondered if Christina had enjoyed the same welcome and her smile dimmed a little.

Sensing her withdrawal, Lucas looked directly into her eyes. 'What's wrong? Tired?'

'No, I just wondered how many other Karadines brides got to do this walk,' she replied flippantly.

'You're the first,' he conceded wryly. 'I should have added if we don't have a tradition we invent one.'

Amber's head jerked around and she looked at him with open-mouthed incredulity. 'You invent...' And staring into his sparkling eyes, she shook her head and grinned.

Hand in hand they walked up the winding path that led to the big rambling Greek-style house. Scarlet bougainvillaea made a brilliant splash of colour against one of the white walls. As they drew closer Amber could see the huge iron gates were open onto the forecourt with an ornate fountain in the centre.

'Come on, let me show you the house.' Lucas urged her inside out of the sun.

'I have been here before,' she reminded him easily.

He looked down at her, his dark glance moving intently over her lovely face. 'As a visitor years ago. Now I welcome you to your home, Amber.'

'And was it Christina's home as well?' She wanted to bite her tongue the minute she'd said it. But to her astonishment Lucas grinned and swept her up high in his arms.'

'Never,' he said adamantly. 'Christina was a city girl through and through. Nothing would persuade her to visit the island. But it's good to know you are jealous.'

Whatever she might have said was lost, as Lucas turned to introduce her to a plump lady waiting in the cool of the interior.

'This is Anna, she keeps the place running. If you want anything you just ask. She does speak a little English.'

Anna shook hands with Amber enthusiastically. 'Welcome, welcome. It is hot for you. You like a cool drink? Lemon?'

'Yes, thank you.' Amber looked around her. The impressive reception hall with its central marble staircase looked different, but she could not immediately think why. She turned enquiring eyes up at Lucas. 'It is different,' she said. 'But why?'

'Let me show you.' Grasping her hand in his again, he gestured with his free hand to ornate double doors set in one wall. 'Remember the sitting room? It has been extended into what was the study. The dining room, the terrace and everything else is the same. But I've had the opposite side extended by about thirty feet.' Then she realised the one wall of the hall that had been blank now had two doors set into it. He led her through one of them.

Amber stared around her in amazement. Pride of place went to a custom-made oak desk fitted with all the latest computer equipment. A long low cream hide sofa overlooked a large window that opened onto a vast expanse of lawn, and in the distance there was what looked like a stone patio area. She turned to look up at Lucas. 'This is your new study,' she surmised.

'No.' He folded his arms around her waist, his black eyes holding hers. 'This is *your* study. I know how much your work means to you and this study has everything you need to keep in touch with the world markets, and your office in London. Mine is next door. I did think of having one big study, but I realised if we shared one neither of us would get much work done. Do you like it?'

Like it! She loved it. Lowering her eyes from his, she swallowed the lump of emotion lodged in her throat. More importantly, she loved what it represented. Years ago he had objected to her work, and now he had done this for her. He was not quite the male chauvinist pig she had thought him to be. He understood her need to work, to be her own woman. Hope grew in her heart for their marriage. Building a study for her was not the act of a man who expected to be rid of her a few months later.

'Well?' he prompted when she took too long to answer.

'I love it,' she said simply. She could feel the threatening prickle of moisture in her eyes, and to hide her emotions she eased out of his embrace and walked back to the window and stared out.

'I knew you would.' Lucas followed, slipping a casual arm around her waist.

Amber leant into him, revelling in the hard heat of his body. 'And of course you are always right,' she teased.

'Not always.' He moved to her side, his eyes catching hers again. 'But I am trying, I want you to be happy here...' he lifted one hand, so he could gently comb his fingers through her long loose hair '...with me,' he husked and she trembled, her breasts swelling against her top.

'I think I will be,' she murmured, wallowing in the wonderful heady sense of elation she was experiencing as she stroked a hand up over his broad chest and felt his muscles ripple with pleasure.

'Good.' His black eyes moved lazily over her small face, the expression in the darkening depths anything but good; wickedly sexual, more like.

'Anna will be here any second,' Amber said, reading his mind.

'You're right.' Lucas grinned, stepping back. 'But I shall continue the guided tour until we reach the bedroom.' Looking out of the window, he added, 'There is no sea view, which is a plus for a study, as it would only be a distraction.' He indicated with his hand the patio area. 'But you do have a view of the heliport so you will know the moment I arrive home.'

Amber couldn't help but burst out laughing. Trust Lucas! He had given her a high-tech study so she could continue to work, but made absolutely sure she would know the second he was home. He hadn't changed that much after all...

'What's so funny?' One dark brow arched in genuine puzzlement.

'Nothing—nothing at all,' Amber said, shaking her head, her long golden hair shimmering over her shoulders.

Anna entered the room carrying a tray with the jug of lemonade and two glasses and, thanking the housekeeper, Amber filled the glasses and handed one to Lucas. 'Drink your lemonade and show me the bedrooms.'

His black eyes flared and he drank down the lemonade in one go. Reaching out to flick her hair back over her shoulder, he implored her to hurry up. Five minutes later he was lowering her down onto an enormous bed, and joining her.

'Nice bedroom,' Amber commented, running her fingers up into his hair, and then his mouth covered hers.

Clothes were ripped off, and with eager hands and hot and urgent mouths they explored and gloried in each other, until finally once more they reached the ultimate pinnacle of passion and then slid languidly into the heated comfort of the aftermath.

'All right, Amber?' Lucas's husky demand vibrated against her smooth cheek, as she lay sprawled on top of him.

'Better than all right,' she breathed against his chest, and, pushing herself up, she looked around. She spied her skirt, her *torn* skirt, and, glancing back down at Lucas, she added, 'But we have to stop doing this or I will very soon have no clothes left!'

'I have to go to Milan next week. Come with me and you can shop till you drop.'

She went to Milan with him, and Lucas bought her a complete new wardrobe, and on returning to the island she modelled the whole lot for him, including the lingerie, with countless interruptions.

It was lucky she had because over the ensuing weeks Lucas spent only three days a week in Athens, but numerous business colleagues arrived on the island. Though she had told herself she would not socialise, she did, and she was too much of a professional to greet smart-suited businessmen in cut-off jeans. She contacted her own office and discovered quite a few of her clients had insisted on dealing only with her. With the compliance of her boss, and the state-of-the-art equipment Lucas had provided, she quickly slipped back into work mode and when Lucas was in Athens she spent the time as hard at work.

As the weeks stretched into two months they developed an enviable lifestyle. They went swimming, sailed, ate together and slept together. They also talked, listened to music or sometimes simply sat companionably in the same room reading. The one thing they did not do was talk about their relationship and underpinning all their activities was the simmering desire for each other. Their love-making was great. They could not keep their hands off each other.

Amber wandered out onto the terrace and sat down on a conveniently placed lounger overlooking the gardens and the pool, and stared out at the sun-drenched blue of the sea beyond. Her marriage was working better than she had ever dreamed possible. She remembered their early-morning romp and a sensual smile curved her wide mouth. But was sex enough? she asked herself, chewing her bottom lip with her teeth. It was Monday and three weeks today she was supposed to return to England. She would have to go back anyway, because, although she could keep on top of her job as well from the island as England, her clients expected some personal contact, as did the other partners in the firm. She would miss this place, lazing around in only briefs and a cotton shirt, with the greatest lover in the world for company. What more could a woman want?

'Hi, beautiful, waiting for me?' Lucas leant over and brushed his lips lightly over her brow before sitting down on the lounger beside her, flicking open the buttons of his jacket and shrugging it off.

'Yes. But I didn't hear the helicopter.' Amber glanced across at him, and watched as he unfastened the buttons of his shirt and lay back with a sigh. He had been in Athens today and he looked tired—sexy but tired.

With his eyes closed, his long lashes curled on high cheekbones, his firm lips curved in a smile. 'That's because I came back by boat. The helicopter is out of service until Saturday.'

'But what about the rest of the week?'

Lucas dealt her a simmering look from half-closed eyes. 'The rest of the week, I am going to stay here with you.'

Amber rose to her feet and, leaning over him, she murmured, 'Promises, promises.' She pressed her lips to his, probing his mouth with her tongue. Lucas responded by slipping his strong hands up under the soft shirt she was wearing to cup her full, firm breasts with his palms, and groaning. 'This is what I came back for,' he confided hoarsely, and moments later they were in the shuttered coolness of their bedroom.

Amber threw off her shirt, and watched utterly enslaved as Lucas stripped off his, and then with a husky growl tumbled her naked onto the bed.

A long powerful thigh nudged hers apart and she wrapped her arms around his neck and kissed his mouth, his eyes, his shoulder, anywhere she could reach.

His long fingers teased her nipples, traced over her stomach and parted the soft folds of velvety flesh between her thighs. Amber groaned out loud, heat flooding through her, and he took her hard and fast, and she was with him all the way until their mingled cries of release left them absolutely sated in each other's arms.

'Do you think the hot climate in Greece has anything to do with making people feel sexy?' Amber asked lazily.

A great guffaw of laughter greeted her remark, and Lucas, propping himself up on one elbow, stared down at her. 'You know what I l...' And he stopped, an arrested expression in his black eyes. He focused on her flushed face, her swollen mouth, thick black lashes screening his gaze. 'What I adore about you, Amber, for all your brains and beauty, you can be so naive.'

Amber forced a grin to her lips, but for a moment there she had been sure he was going to say he loved her. 'Better naive than world-weary, like some I could mention.'

He didn't rise to her teasing but looked at her for a long while with disturbing intensity. 'You're right.' And, rolling off the bed, Lucas strolled over to the bathroom. 'I need a shower.'

Ah, well! Amber sighed happily. They had the whole week together. But she was wrong...

After dinner Lucas retired to his study to make a few calls and Amber headed for bed. Fifteen minutes later, showered and wearing a peach-coloured satin negligée, Amber walked back into the bedroom, the material floating around her as she moved. Tiny shoestring straps supported the bodice—a delicately embroidered web of fine lace revealing tantalising glimpses of her full breasts and dusky nipples. Outrageously sexy, it had been chosen for her by Lucas and Amber felt great wearing it. She crossed to the dressing table, and, opening a drawer, withdrew the small box that held her contraceptive pills, a dreamy smile on her face. Lucas would be joining her soon. Flipping open the top of a delicately lacquered box, she picked up a pill and lifted her hand to her mouth.

'What the hell are you doing?' Lucas's deep voice roared, and the box went flying through the air, pills cascading on the floor, and suddenly her wrist was caught in an iron grip. 'Drop it. Drop it now,' he said in a rough threatening voice, with menace in his dark eyes.

The single pill fell from her fingers, and Amber felt a frisson of fear run down her spine. She had never seen Lucas in such a violent temper.

He pulled her towards him, the strong dark planes of his face contorted with rage. 'What are they?' he demanded, fury in every line of his body. 'Tell me, damn you.'

She opened her mouth to speak but no sound came out. The tension in him was so strong that she shivered at the impact of it. She stared at him, and the violence leaping in his eyes scared her witless. Amber told herself she had no reason to fear him, she had every right to take birth control pills.

'Answer me, woman,' he raged, his hand falling from her hair to curve around her throat, tipping her head back. 'Tell me or so help me I'll—'

'You're hurting me.' She choked, the breath squeezed from her lungs.

Suddenly he released her, but he still held her wrist. She tried to jerk away, shaking from head to foot, but he forcibly pulled her closer.

'Birth control pills,' she muttered in a low, frightened voice.

'Not amphetamines,' Lucas grated between his teeth, some of the anger easing from his body. 'You're sure?' His simmering black eyes fixed on her face.

Some opinion he had of her that he dared suggest she would take drugs. Anger tightened her mouth, and she returned his look with a hard, level stare. 'They are my birth control pills,' she reiterated.

'My wife, and you—'

'Thought I was a junkie,' Amber cut in hardly.

She saw him stiffen 'One cannot be too sure nowadays.' His dark eyes were hooded and curiously blank when he added, 'You'd better pick them up, as you seem to think you need them.' Letting go of her wrist, he spun around and stalked off into the bathroom without another word.

Amber crawled around the floor trying to find her remaining pills, and then, placing the box back in the drawer, she climbed into bed. Lucas's reaction puzzled her—it had been out of all proportion, and totally out of character.

The bathroom door opened and Lucas approached the bed, a small white towel flung precariously around his hips, and with another towel he was rubbing his damp hair. Helplessly Amber's eyes trailed over his magnificent tanned torso, and she forgot their brief argument, her body warming at the sight of him.

Lucas slid into bed and, leaning over her, brushed a few strands of hair from her forehead, his fingertips stroking down the curve of her cheek. 'Do you like children, Amber?'

'Yes,' she murmured, but warning bells rang in her brain.

'So why the pill? You're a married woman,' he asked silkily, his dark eyes intent and a little speculative on her lovely face.

Amber didn't want this conversation, not now, not yet... Easing away from his side, she looked up at him, and, choosing her words carefully, she said, 'You told me to take it the first time we were together, so naturally I do now.'

'And if I told you to stop? If I told you I wanted you to be the mother of my child,' he suggested, 'how would you respond?'

Her heart missed a beat, but her own sense of self-preservation made her cautious. 'That it was not a very sensible suggestion if we are to part in a few months.' She waited with bated breath, hoping and praying for him to ask her to stay for ever, tell her he cared. She was disappointed...

For a space of ten seconds he didn't speak. She saw the muscles bunch at the edge of his jaw, and if she had not known better she would have thought he was shocked. 'That could be ignored,' he finally offered.

'Why?' She had to know. She had swallowed her pride once where Lucas was concerned and she wasn't doing it a second time. It was his turn...

'I'm forty-one, it is time I had a family, and you are twenty-nine next week. It makes sense.'

There was nothing in the world she wanted more than to have his baby, but the cold calculation in his words and his unsubtle reminder of her age were not what she had wanted to hear and her disappointment was intense. 'I'll take it under consideration,' she mocked, evading a direct answer. 'But right now, I'm tired, can we have this conversation some other time?'

'There is nothing more to say.' Amber flinched at the finality in his tone, the cold derision in the eyes that met hers, and when he turned his back on her and went to sleep she had a sinking feeling the honeymoon was over.

Wednesday afternoon she answered the telephone in her study, and smiled at the sound of her father's voice. She needed something to cheer her up, as her marriage was going down the pan fast. Yesterday Lucas had buried himself away in his study, only surfacing for meals. Last night they had lain in the same bed, but as far apart as it was possible to be. Amber could sense him both physically and mentally withdrawing from her and she could do nothing about it. But realistically she knew a relationship built only on sex was bound to fail. The only question was *when*?

Five minutes of listening to all the city and family gossip cheered her up.

'We had visitors at the weekend—your friend Clive.' Her father chuckled.

'Clive?' Amber responded in surprise.

'Yes, he wanted to know if you will be back for your birthday next week.'

'Not next week, but I will be back soon.' Amber didn't see Lucas standing at the open door of her study or the murderous expression on his face as he turned and left. A few minutes later she concluded the conversation.

Turning back to the computer, she tried to work. The

mood Lucas was in there was no point in joining him, she thought acidly.

'Are you busy?' The man occupying her thoughts walked into the room.

Amber swung around on her chair. 'Not if you can think of something better to do,' she teased with determined cheerfulness. He was wearing a beige linen suit, and the desperate thought occurred to her that, if she got him almost naked in the pool, perhaps they could get back to the way they had been. 'It's so hot I thought I might go for a swim.' Rising to her feet, she walked towards him.

'Don't let me stop you,' he said bitingly. Her golden gaze winged to his and she froze at the contempt she saw in his black eyes.

'I thought you might join me,' she said quietly.

His mouth twisted into a mockery of a smile. 'Sorry, but I have to go to Athens after all, something has come up.'

'I thought the helicopter—'

'It is repaired,' he said, cutting her off. Anger gleamed cold as ice in the darkness of his eyes, but there was reluctant desire too, and it was the desire she responded to when he pulled her into his arms and kissed her with a fierce, possessive passion. Then just as fiercely he put her away from him.

'I won't be back until Saturday. If you need anything, call me—Tomso has the number.' He strode out of the room.

What she needed he could not give her, she realised with a despairing sigh, the sound lost in the whirring sound of the helicopter arriving. He had not even said goodbye.

Amber watched from the window as the helicopter rose

in the air and vanished. It was happening all over again—Lucas running out on her. The truly sad part was, Amber realised stoically, she wasn't even surprised she had no faith in him. She'd been expecting it.

CHAPTER ELEVEN

AFTER spending the night alone, Amber was nowhere near as stoic. She missed Lucas desperately. She had not slept. She couldn't work, and finally mid-morning she decided to walk down to the pier. Tomso waved her into the bar and over a cup of coffee he rhapsodised in fractured English over Lucas and their marriage, informing her they had never seen Lucas so happy, and if anyone deserved to be happy he did after the terrible loneliness of the past few years.

Amber presumed Tomso meant the deaths of all Lucas's family members and it made her think. She had acquired a whole new family that had taken her into their home and hearts while Lucas had lost his. His grief must have been horrendous. Strolling back along the beach, she sat down on the hot sand and took a long, hard look at herself, and was not impressed at what she saw.

She claimed she loved Lucas, but she was too proud and too frightened of being hurt to tell him. But she was hurting now anyway. If she truly loved him, and she did, she should be declaring it from the rooftops, not hiding it as though it were something shameful. Was she really so lacking in courage?

As for Lucas, he had an inherent need to be in control at all times. He was a dynamic, arrogant man, but not a man to talk about his feelings or show them. He was a loner; he withdrew behind a cool, aloof mask at the least sign of challenge to his real emotions. Yet when they made love Amber was almost sure he was as overwhelmed as

171

she was, but far too proud to admit it. But then so was she…

Lucas had hinted she stay with him and have his child. Perhaps that was as near as he could get to admitting he wanted her every way a man wanted a woman, and not just as the sex object he had once labelled her. Christina was dead, and Amber was pretty certain there was no other woman in his life. Dared she take a chance and tell him how she felt? Was she strong enough to cope if he rejected her love? The answer to both questions was yes.

The bible said, 'hope deferred maketh the heart sick,' and it was happening to her. Surely it was better to know the truth one way or the other and get on with her life? And, with that thought in mind, she had made her decision.

The following morning Amber dressed with care in one of her Milan purchases. A sleek white linen dress, with a slightly scooped neckline, buttoned from top to bottom and skimming her slender body from shoulder to mid-thigh, with a matching fabric high-heeled sandals and shoulder-bag to complete the outfit. Her long hair was swept up in a twist on top of her head, and even in the late summer heat she looked coolly sophisticated. She had talked Tomso into bringing her to the mainland by boat and he had also arranged the taxi to carry her to the tower block that housed the offices of Karadines International.

Getting out of the taxi, she hitched her bag on her shoulder and took a step towards the entrance and froze. She blinked and blinked again. It couldn't be—she was seeing things. The woman was dead…

'Amber, it's good to see you again. I was sorry to hear about Spiro, but I hear congratulations are in order, and, hey, Lucas isn't a bad old stick. Even after our divorce he still looks after me, though he does not have to. We have just been to see him.'

It was Christina, a slim, beautiful, positively glowing with life Christina, and obviously pregnant, accompanied by a very handsome young man whom she proudly introduced as her husband with love shining in her dark eyes.

The blood drained from Amber's face. She was pole-axed. She said something and it must have been okay, because a few minutes later she was standing on her own, her dazed eyes watching Christina and her husband walk down the street.

'Hi, Amber.' She vaguely heard her name and turned her head; it was Joe. 'Are you okay? You look like you've seen a ghost.'

'Maybe I have,' she said without thinking in her shocked state, her stomach twisted with nausea and sweat dampening her smooth brow.

'Funny! I'm glad to see you haven't lost your sense of humour. Lucas has been acting like a bear with a sore head for the last two days. For the sake of his poor beleaguered workforce, try and cheer him up, will you? You are going up to see him?

'Oh, yes.' See him! She was going to kill him... Lucas had lied...

'Come. I'll show you to his private lift.' With Joe leading the way, Amber stalked into the Karadines building. Joe ushered her into the small lift.

'It opens into his private office suite. I'll probably catch you later,' Joe said with a grin as the doors swished shut.

Amber sank back against the wall, her mind a mass of teeming emotional pain, humiliation, sheer disbelief. It was a horrible thought, but until now she had not realised how much she had counted on Christina being finally out of his life to win Lucas's love. Tim had told her to take a chance, but she had never had one... Lucas had told her his wife was dead. It was a lie of such magnitude no one

with any sense of morality could forgive it. Not only was
Christina alive and well, but she had divorced Lucas and
married a gorgeous young man and was pregnant. But
Lucas was still looking after her.

With blinding clarity Amber saw it all. It must have
been a hell of a jolt to Lucas's colossal ego to be rejected
by the woman he loved, the woman who had lost his child,
and then to see Christina happily married and pregnant
again.

Amber had felt sympathy for him and had hoped that
once the grieving was past he would fall in love with her.
Only last night she'd decided to tell him how much she
loved him, and all the time the swine had lied to her. His
request she have his baby took a much more sinister turn
in the light of Christina's pregnancy. Lucas hated to lose
at anything. If his ex-wife could have another child, then
so could he. Lucas didn't care about her, Amber realised.
She was obviously a convenient pawn to be used in the
competition with his ex-wife, and Spiro's legacy was an
added bonus.

Amber had been second best once in Lucas's life and
she was damned if she would be again. She didn't need
the lying, conniving pig, and she was about to tell him so.
By the time the lift stopped Amber's overriding emotion
was murderous rage.

Her golden eyes leaping with fury, she strode out of the
lift, and on past a stunned-looking secretary who cried,
'You can't go in there,' as Amber thrust wide the door of
Lucas's office, and slammed it shut behind her.

The object of her fury was sitting behind a large desk.
His head shot up as the door slammed, his black brows
arching enquiringly, and not a flicker of emotion disturbed
his hard-cut handsome features. 'Amber, to what do I owe
this honour?'

'Honour, honour!' she screeched, striding across to the desk and planting her hands flat on it. 'You don't know the meaning of the word, you devious, lying bastard.'

'Be careful what you say, Amber.' Lucas shoved back his seat and stood up, moving around the desk. 'A Greek will not allow anyone to cast a slur on his honour. Even you, my beautiful virago,' he drawled mockingly, but with a hint of steel in his tone.

'How could you?' she demanded wildly. 'How could you tell me Christina was dead? What kind of sick joke was that? You want to get down on your knees and pray for your immortal soul or you will surely go to hell.' She was in full flood now. Her golden gaze clashed with his. 'The night before our wedding Tim convinced me to take a chance on you growing to love me. After all, you were a man with a man's need and your first wife was dead. So I did.' Amber didn't see the brilliant flare of triumph in Lucas's eyes—she was on a roll. 'The other night when you flung my pills from my hand...' she accompanied the word with the gesture, knocking a desk lamp flying to the floor with a resounding crash, but even that did not stop her '...then you suggested I have your baby, I, idiot that I am, actually felt guilty for denying you. I spent all yesterday thinking how really you were a caring guy, but too shy to show your emotions!' A hysterical laugh escaped her. 'Shy! You don't have any genuine emotions, only devious plans!'

'Amber,' Lucas slotted in, 'you've got it all wrong.' Reaching out, he grasped her upper arms.

'No. I have finally got it right! After five long, miserable years I am over you. I actually came here today to tell you the opposite. What a joke! I got out of the taxi and, low and behold, risen from the dead on your doorstep I meet Christina, the woman you really love. God! How it must have dented your pride to have your young wife discard you. But I am through being a substitute for any woman.'

'Shut up and listen to me.' His hands tightened on her arms. 'You're screaming like a fish wife, and there is no need.'

His eyes were black but there was fire in them that mirrored the violent emotion in her own. 'Need. What would you know about need? Everything is sex and money to you,' she retorted, trying to pull free, but his grip tightened.

Suddenly aware of how close they were, she felt a trembling start deep in the pit of her stomach, and she stared at him in blazing, humiliating anger. 'I am through listening to you,' she said, feeling her hands clenching into fists at her sides. 'I am leaving you. I never want to see you again. As for Spiro's legacy, see my lawyer.'

His mouth curled in a chilling smile. 'Very convincing but don't pretend you're leaving on my account. I heard you yesterday on the telephone talking to Clive, telling him *not next week but soon*. Three nights without sex too long for you, Amber?' he asked with biting sarcasm.

Her hand flew out and slapped his face in blazing anger. His head jerked back and his eyes leaping with rage clashed with hers for a second, before he hauled her hard against him, his mouth crashing down on hers, kissing her with a raw, savage fury that left her with the taste of blood in her mouth.

She tried to struggle, but he was too strong, and when he finally lifted his head she stared at him with bitter, pain-filled eyes, tears burning at the back of her throat because his last crack had told her his opinion of her had never changed. She froze in his arms and pride alone made her tell him the truth.

'I spoke to my father yesterday. He mentioned Clive

had visited him, and as a friend asked if I was coming back for my birthday. A *friend* that is all Clive has ever been. But you,' she said, her lips trembling, 'you never saw me as anything but an easy lay. You have the mind of a sewer rat.' The tears she had restrained for so long filled her eyes; she blinked furiously, but one escaped down the soft curve of her cheek. 'And I am leaving you.' She tried to push him away, the tears falling faster now as the trauma of the last few days, few months, finally caught up with her and Lucas's callous comment had been the last straw.

'Oh, hell, Amber.' Lucas groaned, hauling her tight against him. 'Don't cry. I can't bear to hear you cry.' With one strong hand he stroked her back, while his other hand lifted to her face and his fingers smoothed the wetness from her cheeks.

She choked back a sob. 'I am not crying,' she murmured, but long shudders racked her slender frame.

Suddenly the door opened, and Lucas turned his head and said something violently to his poor secretary, but the interruption gave Amber the strength to break free from him, and, rubbing the moisture from her face, she fought to regain her self-control. She was not shedding another tear over the fiend, and on shaky legs she stepped towards the door.

'No, Amber. Please.' Lucas swept her up in his arms. 'You have had your say, now it is my turn.'

'What do you think you're doing? Put me down,' she demanded hoarsely.

'What I should have done years ago, but never had the guts,' Lucas admitted and, sitting down on the sofa, he held her fast in the cradle of his arms. His face was only inches away from hers, and the black eyes caught hers with brilliant intensity.

Even in her abject misery, to her horror, the scent, the heat of him invaded her senses, reawakening the familiar awareness she always felt in his presence. 'Let me go, Lucas. Your secretary.' She was grasping at any excuse; she had to get away.

'No, I am going to keep you here until you hear me out,' Lucas informed her bluntly. 'Even a condemned man is allowed to speak.' His features were harsh, brooding as he studied her tear-streaked face.

She nodded—she did not trust herself to speak. Better to hear him out and get out, before she broke down completely in front of him.

'Forgive me for what I said about three days without sex. I didn't mean it. But to hear the mention of Clive's name is enough to drive me insane with jealousy.'

He was jealous, and it gave her hope.

'But I believe you, I know you have to go back to London. You love your work, and I had every intention of taking you. I even got your father to purchase the old rectory for us in the village near his home. I thought we could split the year between Greece and England.' And tilting her chin with one finger, he looked deep into her tear-washed eyes. 'But I wanted it to be a surprise for your birthday.'

Surprised! She was amazed. 'You bought a house?' she murmured. He had been planning for their future together, including her career.

He nodded and continued. 'But I don't believe you meant what you said about Christina. Would you really wish her dead? Because that is what you implied.'

'No, never.' She found her voice. Horrified to think how callous she must have sounded. Then she remembered why she had behaved as she had. 'But you lied.'

'I never lied, Amber. That day in your office I told you

my father had died, and Christina had gone the next year. Perhaps my grasp of English is at fault, but since when had *gone* meant the same as *dead*?'

'Then why did you not tell me you were divorced?' she demanded huskily.

'What man wants to discuss the biggest mistake of his life,' he said slowly, and she felt his muscular body lock with tension, 'with the woman he loves?'

She was held in his protective arms, with the warmth of him surrounding her, and for him to suggest he loved her was the cruellest cut of all to her bruised heart. 'Please, Lucas, no more lies: you loved Christina, you told me so. You probably still do,' she said sadly.

His dark eyes locked on hers as if they would see into her very soul. 'No, I lied to you and myself, and I paid for it with the worst few years of my life.' His dark eyes clouded with remembered pain. 'It was my own fault, but the worst part is knowing in my arrogance I hurt you.'

He brushed her lips with his in a bittersweet tenderness that squeezed her heart. This was Lucas as she had never seen him before. 'I got over it,' she muttered.

'You should not have had to.' He eased her off his lap onto the sofa beside him as if she were the most fragile Dresden doll, and placed an arm around her shoulders, holding her turned towards him. 'I need to explain why I behaved the way I did.' His dark eyes clouded with painful memories. 'My mother was a stunningly beautiful woman.' Amber could believe that. Just look at her son!

'Men adored her. She had numerous affairs—her last one ended at her death of a drug overdose when I was thirteen.' Amber gasped—she had not known that.

'Yes, not very pleasant.' Lucas's lips twisted cynically. 'Though the man we were living with at the time was quite good about it. He gave me a thousand drachmas, and told me I was big enough to look after myself and not to think of my mother as a drug addict because she wasn't. She did not need to get high to be the sexiest lady around.'

'It must have been hard for you.' Amber was shocked, the image of Lucas as a young boy living such a life filled her soft heart with compassion.

'I don't want your pity, Amber,' he said hardly. 'I don't deserve it because I let my mother colour my relationship with you. I didn't see it at the time, but I realised it when it was too late.'

Amber sat up a little straighter—this insight into Lucas's character was so unexpected she could not help but be moved and she wanted to hear more.

'When you came to the villa the first time, you were not as I remembered. You had metamorphosised into an elegant, gorgeous girl who made no secret of what she wanted. I, to my shame, had asked you simply so I could fool Father into thinking you were Spiro's girl, and—'

'You don't need to explain—I know all about that.' Amber felt the colour rise in her cheeks; she had been blatant in her pursuit of Lucas.

'Of course, Spiro told you. Anyway, when we became lovers, although you were a virgin, you were so eager, so uninhibited, you were everything I had ever fantasised about. I wanted you morning, noon and night, and it angered me. I vowed never to be like my mother—addicted to sex—and yet around you I was. I had no control where you were concerned. The year we were together I deliberately forced myself to stay away from you for longer than I needed to, just to prove a point. Then, when I did come back early, you had no time for me, so I began to blame you. Stupid, I know, but though I enjoyed everything you had to give I convinced myself you were too sexy, too career-minded, too free-spirited to be anything other than a girlfriend. Too like my mother.'

His mother had a lot to answer for, Amber thought bitterly. She had coloured his view on relationships from a very early age. But she made no comment as Lucas continued.

'The odd occasion marrying you crossed my mind, I quickly dismissed the notion, and not least because I would also have had to tell my father you had never been Spiro's girl. And I had implied it to hide the fact he was gay. I was an arrogant, conceited bastard, I admit it. When the chance came to make a deal with Alex Aristides, I leapt at it. My father was delighted, and when I met Christina, I was at the right age to marry.' He shrugged his broad shoulders beneath his tailored white silk shirt. 'I am Greek; we are strong on tradition and family. I had just had an argument with you about work, and Christina appeared as a sweet, malleable female. Someone I could love and look after.'

'This is all very interesting, Lucas,' Amber cut in, 'but I really don't need to hear any more.' She was not sitting listening to him telling her how much he loved Christina yet again, and, rising to her feet, she was abruptly pulled back down onto Lucas's lap.

'Damn it, Amber. I am putting my pride on the line here.' He held her firm on his lap and his mouth swooped down on hers and he kissed her with a driven urgency that awakened the same response in her, so that in seconds she was flat on her back on the sofa with Lucas lying over her.

'I am trying to tell you I love you. I always have, being brutally honest.' He clasped her head between his large hands, forcing her to look at him, his black eyes dark and glittering with emotion. 'I knew the last time we were together in the loft but I wouldn't admit it, not even to myself.' He kissed her again. 'I knew when I walked into your office three months ago. But still I told myself it was just sex. I had behaved abominably towards you, and I didn't think you would give me the time of day, so I forced you into marrying me.'

'You wanted Spiro's shares,' she reminded him.

'You think so?' His mouth quirked in self-derision as he continued, 'I already have most of them, as you will discover when you hear from the lawyers. You knew Spiro—did you honestly think he would be able to hang onto his inheritance for one year, never mind five? He invested in every crackpot scheme his friends suggested, and then some. At least a dozen times he sold me blocks of his stock.'

'What, you tricked me?' Wide-eyed, she stared at him, her thoughts in chaos.

'Another lie.' His jaw clenched. 'Haven't you realised yet? I would lie, I would cheat, I would do anything to have you.' Lucas groaned, burying his head in the glorious gold hair. 'But, God help me, Amber, I do love you.'

If he did not marry her for Spiro's legacy, then... Amber reached up to him, her slender fingers lacing around the back of his neck, the blood pounding through her veins. 'I think I am beginning to believe you,' she whispered, incredulous hope growing in her heart.

'Spiro's will gave me the excuse to see you again. I took one look at you sitting behind the desk in your office, and I was determined to have you back in my life. When you told me you might marry Clive I was frantic. I freely admit I lied to get you back. I wasn't taking any chances.'

'But you told me you loved Christina.' Amber could not get over that fact. 'I saw you with her in New York—

when she was pregnant you were so crazy about her you asked me to go and look after her.'

A harsh laugh escaped him. 'I had to look after her, but I never loved her. The marriage was over before the honeymoon finished. You can guess what I discovered on my wedding night, you had already hinted as much. But that did not matter. I tried to make the marriage work, though we were rarely together because she refused to travel. Until I discovered the final irony when she was pregnant, and then the gods really laughed at me. Christina was a drug addict, and had been since the tender age of fourteen, which is why she would not go to the island. Too far away from her supplier and, as for sex, she would do anything with anyone for a fix. I never touched her again.'

'Oh, my God, no.' Amber tightened her arms around him, feeling his anguish as if it were her own. 'The night of the party she was rolling her own cigarettes and I wondered why,' she murmured out loud. 'Her little vice, she said.'

'Cannabis was the least of her addictions. Our baby was stillborn two months before the due date because Christina had been taking heroine all along.' Lucas ran a hand over his eyes as if they hurt him.

'And Christina now?' Amber asked.

'I look after her business interests—a promise I made to her father, but I divorced her as soon as my father died. I persuaded her to go into rehab. She met her new husband there. He is a doctor and much more competent to look after her than I. She has been clean for over a year.'

'I see.' Amber looked deep into his night-black eyes and she knew he was telling the truth.

'Do you? Do you really?' His sensuous lips tightened in a grim line. 'Have you any idea what it did to me the other night seeing you with a pill in your hand? Just a few hours earlier I had almost told you that I loved you, and I had to walk away because I suddenly realised the enormity of my mistake. I did not deserve you. You gave me your love once with all the joyous abandonment of a true innocent and I in my arrogance took it as my due and walked out on you for the sake of what I thought would be an easy marriage. I stood in the shower and I could not believe how blind I had been. Then later when I saw the pill in your hand I nearly died. I thought you were on drugs, and after the last few months together I could not live if anything happened to you. When I realised it was a birth control pill I was relieved but I was angry—I wanted you to have my child, but I had not the courage to tell you I loved you. The next day, hearing you talk to Clive, I was gutted.' The expression in his eyes nearly stopped her heart, so full of anguished love that it was almost painful.

'You do love me,' she whispered, hardly daring to believe it was true.

'Believe it.' And he lowered his head, his mouth finding hers in a kiss of aching tenderness. 'You are in my blood, my bones.' His throatily murmured words made Amber tremble inside. She looked up into his darkly handsome face and was stunned by the slight vulnerability in night-black eyes. 'Forgive me, Amber, stay with me, and I swear I will spend the rest of my life trying to win your love.'

'I forgive you, and you won't have to.' Amber smiled. She had a better understanding of why he had behaved the way he had in the past, and if their marriage was to work she had to believe in him, trust him. She moved sinuously against him, her hands reaching up to clutch at his broad shoulders. 'I do love you, Lucas. I always have and always will—there has never, ever been anyone else for me,' she confessed, and pulled his head back down to hers. Her tongue touched his and she felt the shuddering intensity of his response.

They kissed and clung to each other, and with shaking fingers Lucas unfastened the buttons down the front of her dress, and parted the fabric exposing the near naked length of her to his view. 'You are so beautiful, so exquisite inside and out,' he grated, shrugging off his clothes and dispensing with her briefs in seconds. His great body arched over her, his eyes glittered down into hers. 'And you really are all mine at last.' Then his head swooped down, and his mouth covered hers in a kiss of pure possession before burning a red-hot trail of fire down her slender throat to her swollen breasts.

He filled up her senses as never before, she was drunk on the wonder of their declared love. Amber moaned as he found the rosy peaks and licked them with his tongue. Her seeking hands stroked up over his back, traced his spine, and her nails dug into his flesh as he suckled the rigid tips each in turn, until Amber cried out and her back arched involuntarily seeking more.

Lifting his head, he looked down at her. 'I love you, Amber,' Lucas groaned, his voice thick with hunger. 'I want you.' His fingers spread over her flat stomach, caressing all the erotic places he knew so well.

'And I want you always and for ever.'

With a low growl deep in his throat, he slid between her thighs and made her his. With huskily muttered words of love and need, Lucas told her everything she had always wanted to hear fall from his passionate mouth. Their coming together was better than anything that had gone before, because this time their bodies and minds as one added a new dimension. Love.

Surfacing from the exhausted aftermath of their love-making, Amber stirred in Lucas's arms and looked around.

'Get up, Lucas, get off.' She shoved at him and he sat up, allowing her to do the same.

'No regrets, Amber, you are not going to change your mind,' and she was stunned to see a trace of doubt in his slumberous black eyes.

'No.' He loved her, she could feel it in her soul, and she did not like to see her dynamic, powerful husband uncertain. 'But look where we are, is the door locked?' She grabbed the front of her dress and began frantically fastening buttons.

'No.' His dark eyes, brimming with love, held hers. 'But my secretary would not dare disturb us,' he said with all the arrogant confidence Amber recognised.

She smiled. 'I'm taking no more chances,' and, standing up, she continued dressing, glad to see Lucas was doing the same. 'I can't believe we made love in your office.'

Lucas, looking utterly gorgeous with his hair disheveled, his trousers on and his shirt hanging off his shoulders, pulled her into his arms. 'I can, but if it perturbs you so much…' he grinned down at her '…what about trying the rail we missed on the boat? Another honeymoon?'

And they did…

by **Catherine George**

*A family with a passion for life—
and for love.*

Get to know the Dysarts!
Over the coming months you can share
the dramas and joys, and hopes and dreams
of this wealthy English family, as unexpected
passions, births and marriages unfold
in their lives.

LORENZO'S REWARD
Harlequin Presents® #2203
on sale September 2001

RESTLESS NIGHTS
Harlequin Presents® #2244
on sale April 2002

Available wherever Harlequin books are sold.

HARLEQUIN®
Makes any time special ®

Visit us at www.eHarlequin.com　　　　BPADYS

Harlequin truly does make any time special. . . . This year we are celebrating weddings in style!

A Walk Down the Aisle WEDDING CELEBRATION

To help us celebrate, we want you to tell us how wearing the Harlequin wedding gown will make your wedding day special. As the grand prize, Harlequin will offer one lucky bride the chance to **"Walk Down the Aisle"** in the Harlequin wedding gown!

There's more...

For her honeymoon, she and her groom will spend five nights at the **Hyatt Regency Maui.** As part of this five-night honeymoon at the hotel renowned for its romantic attractions, the couple will enjoy a candlelit dinner for two in Swan Court, a sunset sail on the hotel's catamaran, and duet spa treatments.

A HYATT RESORT AND SPA

Maui ▪ Molokai ▪ Lanai

To enter, please write, in, 250 words or less, how wearing the Harlequin wedding gown will make your wedding day special. The entry will be judged based on its emotionally compelling nature, its originality and creativity, and its sincerity. This contest is open to Canadian and U.S. residents only and to those who are 18 years of age and older. There is no purchase necessary to enter. Void where prohibited. See further contest rules attached. Please send your entry to:

Walk Down the Aisle Contest

In Canada
P.O. Box 637
Fort Erie, Ontario
L2A 5X3

In U.S.A.
P.O. Box 9076
3010 Walden Ave.
Buffalo, NY 14269-9076

You can also enter by visiting www.eHarlequin.com
Win the Harlequin wedding gown and the vacation of a lifetime!
The deadline for entries is October 1, 2001.

HARLEQUIN®
Makes any time special ®

PHWDACONT1

HARLEQUIN WALK DOWN THE AISLE TO MAUI CONTEST 1197
OFFICIAL RULES
NO PURCHASE NECESSARY TO ENTER

1. To enter, follow directions published in the offer to which you are responding. Contest begins April 2, 2001, and ends on October 1, 2001. Method of entry may vary. Mailed entries must be postmarked by October 1, 2001, and received by October 8, 2001.

2. Contest entry may be, at times, presented via the Internet, but will be restricted solely to residents of certain geographic areas that are disclosed on the Web site. To enter via the Internet, if permissible, access the Harlequin Web site (www.eHarlequin.com) and follow the directions displayed online. Online entries must be received by 11:59 p.m. E.S.T. on October 1, 2001.

   In lieu of submitting an entry online, enter by mail by hand-printing (or typing) on an 8½" x 11" plain piece of paper, your name, address (including zip code), Contest number/name and in 250 words or fewer, why winning a Harlequin wedding dress would make your wedding day special. Mail via first-class mail to: Harlequin Walk Down the Aisle Contest 1197, (in the U.S.) P.O. Box 9076, 3010 Walden Avenue, Buffalo, NY 14269-9076, (in Canada) P.O. Box 637, Fort Erie, Ontario L2A 5X3, Canada Limit one entry per person, household address and e-mail address. Online and/or mailed entries received from persons residing in geographic areas in which Internet entry is not permissible will be disqualified.

3. Contests will be judged by a panel of members of the Harlequin editorial, marketing and public relations staff based on the following criteria:

   - Originality and Creativity—50%
   - Emotionally Compelling—25%
   - Sincerity—25%

   In the event of a tie, duplicate prizes will be awarded. Decisions of the judges are final.

4. All entries become the property of Torstar Corp. and will not be returned. No responsibility is assumed for lost, late, illegible, incomplete, inaccurate, nondelivered or misdirected mail or misdirected e-mail, for technical, hardware or software failures of any kind, lost or unavailable network connections, or failed, incomplete, garbled or delayed computer transmission or any human error which may occur in the receipt or processing of the entries in this Contest.

5. Contest open only to residents of the U.S. (except Puerto Rico) and Canada, who are 18 years of age or older, and is void wherever prohibited by law; all applicable laws and regulations apply. Any litigation within the Province of Quebec respecting the conduct or organization of a publicity contest may be submitted to the Régie des alcools, des courses et des jeux for a ruling. Any litigation respecting the awarding of a prize may be submitted to the Régie des alcools, des courses et des jeux or for the purpose of helping the parties reach a settlement. Employees and immediate family members of Torstar Corp. and D. L. Blair, Inc., their affiliates, subsidiaries and all other agencies, entities and persons connected with the use, marketing or conduct of this Contest are not eligible to enter. Taxes on prizes are the sole responsibility of winners. Acceptance of any prize offered constitutes permission to use winner's name, photograph or other likeness for the purposes of advertising, trade and promotion on behalf of Torstar Corp., its affiliates and subsidiaries without further compensation to the winner, unless prohibited by law.

6. Winners will be determined no later than November 15, 2001, and will be notified by mail. Winners will be required to sign and return an Affidavit of Eligibility form within 15 days after winner notification. Noncompliance within that time period may result in disqualification and an alternative winner may be selected. Winners of trip must execute a Release of Liability prior to ticketing and must possess required travel documents (e.g. passport, photo ID) where applicable. Trip must be completed by November 2002. No substitution of prize permitted by winner. Torstar Corp. and D. L. Blair, Inc., their parents, affiliates, and subsidiaries are not responsible for errors in printing or electronic presentation of Contest, entries and/or game pieces. In the event of printing or other errors which may result in unintended prize values or duplication of prizes, all affected game pieces or entries shall be null and void. If for any reason the Internet portion of the Contest is not capable of running as planned, including infection by computer virus, bugs, tampering, unauthorized intervention, fraud, technical failures, or any other causes beyond the control of Torstar Corp. which corrupt or affect the administration, secrecy, fairness, integrity or proper conduct of the Contest, Torstar Corp. reserves the right, at its sole discretion, to disqualify any individual who tampers with the entry process and to cancel, terminate, modify or suspend the Contest or the Internet portion thereof. In the event of a dispute regarding an online entry, the entry will be deemed submitted by the authorized holder of the e-mail account submitted at the time of entry. Authorized account holder is defined as the natural person who is assigned to an e-mail address by an Internet access provider, online service provider or other organization that is responsible for arranging e-mail address for the domain associated with the submitted e-mail address. **Purchase or acceptance of a product offer does not improve your chances of winning.**

7. Prizes: (1) Grand Prize—A Harlequin wedding dress (approximate retail value: $3,500) and a 5-night/6-day honeymoon trip to Maui, HI, including round-trip air transportation provided by Maui Visitors Bureau from Los Angeles International Airport (winner is responsible for transportation to and from Los Angeles International Airport) and a Harlequin Romance Package, including hotel accomodations (double occupancy) at the Hyatt Regency Maui Resort and Spa, dinner for (2) two at Swan Court, a sunset sail on Kiele V and a spa treatment for the winner (approximate retail value: $4,000); (5) Five runner-up prizes of a $1000 gift certificate to selected retail outlets to be determined by Sponsor (retail value $1000 ea.). Prizes consist of only those items listed as part of the prize. Limit one prize per person. All prizes are valued in U.S. currency.

8. For a list of winners (available after December 17, 2001) send a self-addressed, stamped envelope to: Harlequin Walk Down the Aisle Contest 1197 Winners, P.O. Box 4200 Blair, NE 68009-4200 or you may access the www.eHarlequin.com Web site through January 15, 2002.

Contest sponsored by Torstar Corp., P.O. Box 9042, Buffalo, NY 14269-9042, U.S.A.

PHWDACONT2

Coming Next Month

HARLEQUIN *Presents*

THE BEST HAS JUST GOTTEN BETTER!

#2199 DUARTE'S CHILD Lynne Graham
Only days before she gave birth, Emily left her husband, Duarte de Monteiro. Now Duarte has traced her and his baby son, and brought them back to Portugal—because he loves her, or just because he wants his son?

#2200 TO MAKE A MARRIAGE Carole Mortimer
Andie is convinced her baby's father is in love with another woman. But Adam Monroe is also a close family friend—Andie knows she can't avoid him forever....

#2201 MISTRESS BY CONTRACT Helen Bianchin
There was only one way for Mikayla to clear her father's debt to tycoon Rafael Velez-Aguilera: offer herself in exchange! Rafael was intrigued by Mikayla's proposal, and immediately specified her duties as his mistress for a year!

#2202 THE ALVARES BRIDE Sandra Marton
No one knew the father of Carin's baby—but during the birth she called out a name: Raphael Alvares! The powerful Brazilian millionaire rushed to Carin's bedside—but had he come because the one passionate night they'd shared had left him longing to make Carin his bride?

#2203 LORENZO'S REWARD Catherine George
When Lorenzo Forli proposed, Jess had no qualms about letting her husband-to-be make passionate love to her. But Lorenzo had failed to tell Jess something about his past. Could it be that he'd used all the means he possessed only to seduce her into his bed?

#2204 TERMS OF ENGAGEMENT Kathryn Ross
In order to avoid her ex-husband, Emma had introduced Frazer McClarren as her new fiancé. Time and time again they were forced to play the happy couple, but Emma could not truly get involved with Frazer—she could never give him what he wanted....

HPCNM0801